I0639586

John O'Keeffe

The London Hermit or Rambles in Dorsetshire

A Comedy as Performed as Performed with Universal Aüpplause at the

Theatres Royal. Fifth Edition

John O'Keeffe

The London Hermit or Rambles in Dorsetshire
A Comedy as Performed as Performed with Universal Aüpplause at the Theatres Royal. Fifth Edition

ISBN/EAN: 9783744767880

Printed in Europe, USA, Canada, Australia, Japan

Cover: Foto ©Andreas Hilbeck / pixelio.de

More available books at **www.hansebooks.com**

THE
LONDON HERMIT,

OR,

RAMBLES IN DORSETSHIRE,

A

COMEDY,

AS PERFORMED WITH UNIVERSAL APPLAUSE

AT THE

THEATRES ROYAL.

By *JOHN O'KEEFFE, Esq.*

AUTHOR OF

Tony Lumpkin in Town, The Son-in-law, The Dead Alive, Agreeable Surprize, Caftle of Andalufia, Fontainbleau, or Our Way in France, The Pofitive Man, The Poor Soldier, Love in a Camp, or Patrick in Pruffia, The Farmer, The Young Quaker, Beggar on Horfeback, Peeping Tom, The Prifoner at Large, The Toy, or Hampton Court Frolics, Wild Oats, or the Strolling Gentlemen, Little Hunchback, The Siege of Curzola, Modern Antiques, or the Merry Mourners, The Highland Reel, Birth-Day, or Prince of Arragon, Sprigs of Laurel, Life's Vagaries, Irifh Mimic, or Blunders at Brighton, &c.

FIFTH EDITION.

LONDON:
Printed for J. BARKER, *Dramatic Repofitory*, Ruffell-Court,
Drury-Lane. 1798.   [Pr. 1s 6d]

Where the following Pieces by Mr. O'Keeffe are publifhed:

Life's Vagaries.----Irifh Mimic.----Little Hunchback.----Birth-Day.----
Oatlands, an Ode.----Tony Lumpkin in Town.

DEDICATION.

TO THE

Rev. —— BALL, of Winfrith,
Near Weymouth.

DEAR SIR,

WHEN I rambled into Dorfetſhire in the ſummer of 1791, my only introduction to your acquaintance was your own frank affability, and my ſole recommendation to your hoſpitable roof, that I was a ſtranger. By your good-natured politeneſs, my mind was cheered in the ſolitudes of Lulworth, and by your many friendly and kind offices I was furniſhed with information in a place where all was novelty,

I   though

though my firſt charm there was the certainty of what I had ſuppoſed to be common in England, a pious and benevolent clergyman; and though I could, previous to my viſits at Winfrith, boaſt the honour of having ſtood before the great gates of a biſhop's palace; yet, for the comforts I there enjoyed in the little parlour of a country parſonage-houſe, accept this trifling teſtimony of well-remembered goodneſs to,

DEAR SIR,

Your highly honoured,

and much obliged ſervant,

J. O'KEEFFE.

BROMPTON,
July 13, 1793.

PROLOGUE.

Written by GEORGE COLMAN, *Jun. Esq.*

Spoken by Mr. BARRYMORE.

DREAD cenfors! by whofe nod we fink or rife!
   Be merry, pray, to-night, and not too wife!
Our bard will fmile at the ftrict critic rule,
He had his learning in a laughing—fchool.
Order, and ancient laws, he dares neglect;
And rather would be pleafant, than correct;
Nay, fpite of all grave claffical communities,
Wou'd fooner make you laugh than keep the uhities.
Mirth is his aim——and critics! we implore you,
Relax, while our light fcenes we lay before you!
Good-humour to the countenance adds graces,
Unbend the iron mufcles of your faces!
Lay acid wifdom by; think mirth no fin;
Throw your four dignity afide,—and grin!
   Yet tho' we laugh we wou'd not quit the grounds
Where fportive nature marks her ample bounds:
Various her range! calm, gay, then in the vapours—
We catch the goddefs while fhe's cutting capers.
To prove that we have caught her in the act,
Our Hermitage is built upon *a fact.*
If, then, the drama's frolic pencil draws   ⎫
A frolic fact—away with critic laws!   ⎬
And grant the fketcher's fancy your applaufe!   ⎭
Oft has he drawn before—this fhop is full
With touches from his hand; and none thought dull;
Should this, to-night, feem vapid to your eyes,
'Twould prove a *Dif-*Agreeable Surprize—
Oh! think on his collection now in ftore,
And fmile on him, on whom you fmil'd before!

DRA-

DRAMATIS PERSONÆ.

M E N.

WHIMMY,	— Mr. SUETT.
OLD PRANKS,	— Mr. AICKIN.
YOUNG PRANKS,	— Mr. BANNISTER, Jun.
PEREGRINE,	— Mr. EVATT.
APATHY,	— Mr. BLAND.
POZ,	— Mr. BARRETT.
BITE,	— Mr. COOKE.
NATTY MAGGS,	— Mr. PALMER, Jun.
BARLEYCORN,	— Mr. BENSON.
TULLY,	— Mr. JOHNSTONE.
SKIP,	— Mr. ABBOT.
BAREBONES,	— Mr. WEWITZER.
TOBY THATCH,	— Mr. PARSONS.
CARTER,	— Mr. BURTON.
JOHN GRUM,	— Mr. ALFRED.
POST BOY,	— Mr. CORNERFORD.
JOHN,	— Mr. LYONS.
COACHMAN,	— Mr. LEDGER.

W O M E N.

DIAN,	— Miss HEARD.
Mrs. MAGGS,	— Mrs. WEBB.
KITTY BARLEYCORN,	— Mrs. KEMBLE.
FISHWOMAN,	— Mrs. POWELL.
LADIES,	— { Mrs. CUYLER. { Mrs. HALE.

SCENE, DORSETSHIRE.

THE

THE

LONDON HERMIT,

OR

RAMBLES in DORSETSHIRE.

ACT I.

SCENE I. *Before a Country Inn and great Gates leading to* Whimmy's *Houſe.*

Enter BARLEYCORN, *(from the Inn.)*

BARLEYCORN.

TOBY, Toby Thatch! what doſt ſtand gaping about there?

Enter TOBY.

Been up hill to look towards great road.

BARLEYCORN.

Any carriages coming?

TOBY.

Fine coach and four horſes---a high thing---O me! chay---a pheaton (I think they call it)---and a whiſ-key-me-gig.

B

B   BARLEY-

BARLEYCORN.

And there's a boat full of company juft put in at the cove, all to fee 'Squire Whimmy's improvements---Then there's our poney-race. Dang my buttons, we fhall have a houfe full to-day. What a donkey was I to let that daughter of mine go gadding to Blandford. Company flocking,---and my child, that ought to have my intereft at heart, when fhe fhou'd be preparing entertainment for the guefts, mayhap, fhe's now gawking over a race-courfe.

TOBY.

And all the bufinefs left upon I.

BARLEYCORN.

Always grumbling, you idle rafcal.

TOBY.

Well, I've more trades than the beft idle rafcal in all England. I'm waiter and attend the company, as oftler I wait on horfes; I paints the names on the fmugglers' boats; I plays the fiddle at church; I'm a tight lockfmith; I'm a bit'n a parifh conftable; and for walking on meffages to Weymouth, Blandford, Corfe, Poole, or Wareham, I'm allow'd to be as fmart a footpad as any in the county of Dorfet. [*Laughing without.*] There's the 'Squire's farvants within, ha! ha! ha!---they've rare ftingo at home, and yet come drinking our taplafh. I'll go farve 'em. *(Going.)*——but there's their mafter come upon 'e ;---he's in a mortifh fury with fom'at.

BARLEYCORN.

Dang my buttons! This daughter of mine not come yet, and here the houfe now chuck full.

TOBY.

I'll run and fee; for I warrants Kitty will bring home fome fine ballads.

BARLEYCORN.

Our fubfcription's not full to buy the filver cup; and the folks are already gaping for the race. Take you the paper about and ax what the company will give towards it.

TOBY.

I wool,   [*Exit.*

Enter WHIMMY, *(in a rage.)*

WHIMMY.

You, firrah! did I not build this inn here for you at the very entrance of my improvements? Did not I put you and your family into it, and an't you getting money here as if you coin'd it? Is it not a bean-garden that I've turn'd you into; and an't you fattening in it, like a bafe ungrateful great boar as you are?

BARLEYCORN.

Great boar! I don't underftand what your honour would be at.

WHIMMY.

Here, on the very day I have propriated to oblige the world of tafte and fafhion, by fhowing them my houfe, pictures, gardens, and improvements, you muft fix your damn'd twopenny poney-race.

BARLEYCORN.

I did it to draw company to the village.

                  WHIMMY.

WHIMMY.

Yes, to your own paltry alehoufe, you fordid rafcal!

BARLEYCORN.

Improvements!---Who'd come to view your improvements, Sir, if they wa'n't fure of a good dinner from me? If they can eat marvel and drink water, they may feaft upon your improvements; but after all their eye-gluttony in your gardens, their palates are ready enough for a Scotch-collop at the Red Lion. Here, you Toby, why don't you mind the company. *(Calling off.)* Dang my buttons!--- Landlord---Big boar---Pay his rent.

[*Exit muttering.*

WHIMMY.

Here's plebeian gratitude!---Oh! plague of the fingers that fign'd you a feven years leafe.

OLD PRANKS *without.*

No, no,---I'll walk up to Whimmy's---Oh! why he's here---How d'ye do, Dick?---Found you out, eh!

WHIMMY.

My name is Richard.---What! the friend of my youth, Billy Pranks.---*(Afide.)* Now fhall I be twitted with former favours; and I don't like that.

OLD PRANKS.

So, you've pick'd up the mocuffes in the Indies! Pack'd up, came over.---Never look'd after me.

WHIMMY.

I afk'd every body after you.

OLD PRANKS.

What! I fuppofe you afk'd King Charles at Cha-ring-Crofs;---Nobody about 'Change could tell of William Pranks, the banker, of Lombard-ftreet.---You hound, I was your friend when you hadn't another; but now you don't want one------

WHIMMY.

Hound, what's the matter with you? Wou'd you have me advertife or fend the bellman about to cry you?

OLD PRANKS.

You're moft plaguily alter'd for the worfe. Well, I've been told all about you.

WHIMMY.

Then, as you have heard I've hopes of a peerage, you might be a little more refpectful, Billy.

OLD PRANKS.

If you want to have more refpect than another man, be better than another man; for your being call'd a lord, can neither give you a wife head or a good heart. How's your daughter? fine girl, I hear; wonder'd at it, when I thought of your phiz.

WHIMMY.

You are as civil as ever.

OLD PRANKS.

You fhall give her to my nephew, the greateft rogue in England.

WHIMMY.

Why there may be finer girls than my daughter, yet I think fhe's too good for a rogue.

OLD

OLD PRANKS.

Where did you make your fortune ?

WHIMMY.

You know in the Indies to be fure. *(Afide.)* If I had millions this fellow ftill overawes me, that I'm a mere moufe before him.

OLD PRANKS.

I fcorn to remind you;---you owe all that fortune to me.

WHIMMY, *(afide.)*

'Twill be long enough before I repay you.

OLD PRANKS.

Only think of all the good things I've done for you. Didn't I fuffer you to write for me from fix in the morning to feven at night; lock'd you up, and fed you upon bread and cheefe, to fharpen your induftry upon the grindftone of neceffity.

WHIMMY.

Yes ; you did keep my nofe to the grindftone.

OLD PRANKS.

Wasn't it I got you out to Bombay in a refpectable line of a guinea-pig ? Didn't I procure the letters to the Governor and general officers ? Didn't I write myfelf, " This young man, the bearer, is a " prudent lad, that will do all your dirty work ?"

WHIMMY.

Certainly, your letter did me great honour.

OLD PRANKS.

Didn't you derive all your intereft from a pamphlet

phlet that I wrote, and gave you the credit of, tho'
I thought 'twou'd bring the author to the pillory?

WHIMMY.

I acknowledge all your goodnefs.

OLD PRANKS.

Then give your daughter to my nephew; they
fhall have every penny I'm worth when I die.

WHIMMY.

Aye; but there's danger of your living a great
while, Billy.

OLD PRANKS.

What! are you afraid of it, you golden calf?

WHIMMY.

Where is your nephew?

OLD PRANKS.

Was in the Temple; is now in the King's Bench;
he doesn't know it, but it's I that keep him there, to
make him, from a dread of confinement, avoid running in debt. Shan't give him two fixpences unlefs
he marries your daughter.

WHIMMY.

Aye; but I've promis'd her to a good young man
in the neighbourhood here, who has made the tour
of Europe. Ah! Mr. Peregrine brought home
tafte enough to lay out my gardens, difpofe my ftatues, and make yon fpot the feat of virtù and ele-
gance.

OLD PRANKS, *(afide.)*

Got his money like a knave, and now gives it
away like a fool.

WHIMMY.

WHIMMY.

Not half an hour fince I actually promis'd Mr. Peregrine that he fhou'd marry her to-morrow.

OLD PRANKS.

But, don't you recollect a prior promife to me? Didn't you engage if you ever made a fortune and had a child, my next a-kin fhou'd have both?

WHIMMY.

Aye; but Peregrine will fhoot me if I break my word to him.

OLD PRANKS.

Break it with me, and I'll cut your wizen.

WHIMMY.

Oh dear! I'm brought into this dilemma by my bad memory. Hark ye, Billy, I'll make Peregrine wait, on pretext that his conftancy muft be tried.--- Yes, I'll fend him to travel again for a feven years.

OLD PRANKS.

Inftead of marriage, let him go to-morrow.

WHIMMY.

Aye; but on his return he'll claim my promife.

OLD PRANKS.

Pfhaw!---his back turn'd, my nephew will be here;---I've already fent for him; Tom's a fprightly blade, monftrous wicked tho'.—This the entrance to your grounds?

WHIMMY.

Yes, I've tranfported Italy into England.

OLD PRANKS.

Italy !

WHIMMY.

Here you'll fee gardens.

OLD PRANKS.

I've a garden at Brixton Caufeway.

WHIMMY.

Such bananas---

OLD PRANKS.

What ! do they boil better with a bit of corn'd beef than a fummer cabbage ?

WHIMMY.

Cabbage ! My hot-houfe !---half a dozen fuch peaches laft Chriftmas ! upon a fum up, the rearing will coft me two guineas a piece.

OLD PRANKS.

For whofe eating ?

WHIMMY.

My own, to be fure.

OLD PRANKS.

Old Nick jump after them ; fwallow in a minute what would have kept a whole family for a twelve-month.

WHIMMY.

Wer'n't they my own ?

OLD PRANKS.

Superfluities are not our own, whilft the poor want common neceffaries. When do you dine ?

C

WHIMMY.

WHIMMY.

Not till to-morrow, becaufe I refign my houfe and improvements to-day to the admiration of a wondering public; but you fhall fup with me, my friend.

OLD PRANKS.

Thank ye.

Enter BARLEYCORN.

BARLEYCORN.

Sir, Parfon Jack be making collections for the poor fufferers that was burnt out there at Minehead. He has fent the paper here, to put down your worfhip's name for a trifle.

WHIMMY.

I wifh Parfon Jack would mind the bufinefs of his own parifh; what have we to do with the poor of another county ?

OLD PRANKS.

Hark ye, Dick Whimmy, in the hour of calamity, the unhappy of every country are our fellow-citizens *(gives money.)* Put that down.

BARLEYCORN.

Your name, Sir ?

OLD PRANKS.

Never mind my name.--- If I can do any good, I don't want to blow a trumpet about it.

WHIMMY.

Eh ! well, as it's a charity, I'll give---

BARLEY-

BARLEYCORN.

How much?

WHIMMY.

I'll give them---As I love to be modeft, put down plain Dick Whimmy, one pound one.

BARLEYCORN.

I'll give it myfelf, and dang me if your fhabby name fhall difgrace our parifh paper. [*Exit.*

OLD PRANKS.

That fellow has a foul.

WHIMMY.

There's a faucy villain.

OLD PRANKS.

Yes; but Dick, a fordid mind finks a man into contempt, though mafter of millions.

WHIMMY.

I defire, Billy, not to hear difagreeable thing will you come up with me now?

OLD PRANKS.

I'll throw on a fhirt.

WHIMMY.

Well, you'll excufe me till fupper.---I muft give Tully, my gardener, his leffon,---and—no hermit got yet! Look! I've advertifed for a man to fit dreffed up as a hermit in the hermitage of my gardens.

OLD PRANKS.

Dick, have a good fupper; remember old times.

C 2   WHIMMY.

WHIMMY.

Yes, I fhall never forget bread and cheefe. [*Exit.*

OLD PRANKS.

Invites every body to fee his gardens, and then the fhy churl fneak out of the way. Tell me of carvings and paintings! I fay the beft part of a gentleman's houfe is his kitchen and wine cellar.

Enter TOBY.

TOBY.

Shall your horfe have any oats, Sir?

OLD PRANKS.

Yes, Sir; but if you pleafe, Sir, I'll fee him eat them myfelf, Sir; for if the poor beaft is cheated, he can't even fummons us to a court of confcience. [*Ex.*

TOBY.

Stand to look at a horfe eating corn! Ecod then you muft be main fond of feeing other folks at dinner. [*Exit.*

Enter YOUNG PRANKS, *and* KITTY BARLEYCORN *in a genteel travelling drefs.*

YOUNG PRANKS.

Have you forgot any thing in the chaife, Ma'am?

KITTY.

Oh dear! yes, (*fearching her pockets.*)

Enter POST BOY.

BOY.

You dropt this.   [*Exit.*

1   KITTY.

KITTY.

Oh Lord! my book of ballads that I bought at Blandford.

YOUNG PRANKS.

A divine girl!---but what the devil does she want with a book of ballads ? *(aside)*---Really Mifs don't you go any farther ?

KITTY.

Why no, Sir.---Lud I hope he won't find out that my father keeps this inn here, *(aside.)*---Sir, I wait here, and expect my friends to fend a fervant and a horfe for me.

YOUNG PRANKS.

Oho! then you're fond of riding, I prefume, Mifs?

KITTY.

Oh, yes, Sir, with a pillion.

YOUNG PRANKS.

Oh!---behind a------Heavens! that I was the happy fervant to ride before you.

KITTY.

Cou'dn't expect a gentleman like you, Sir.--- Dear, I'm afraid my father or Toby will come out to expofe me, *(aside.)* Then, Sir, you're going on to Weymouth ?

YOUNG PRANKS.

Yes, Ma'am, my feet, head, body, and hands, but my foul remains at---What's the name of this village, Mifs ?

KITTY.

I really don't know, Sir,---though I was born in it, (*aside.*)

YOUNG PRANKS.

I wonder, do we change horfes here, or get another chaife?

KITTY.

I fancy, Sir, you change the carriage.---Lud! I wifh it was ready, and he'd go off, though when he's gone, I fhall be indeed unhappy. (*aside.*)

YOUNG PRANKS.

Mifs, won't you take fome refrefhment? we'd beft---ftep in.---Permit me the honour of accompanying you.

KITTY.

(*Afide.*) Oh dear! then he finds out who I am, and will defpife me.---Why no, Sir---my grand papa's fervant may be now waiting, and he's a very crofs crufty grumps, if he'd fee a gentleman with me.

YOUNG PRANKS.

Eh! what's going forward yonder up the hill? a race here, I believe.

KITTY.

Oh! yes, Sir, for the filver cup.---Dear! what a fine thing 'twou'd be for father to win it. Our parlour cuftomers love to drink out of filver.

YOUNG PRANKS.

Cuftomers!

KITTY.

KITTY.

(*Aside, and confused.*) Oh, Lud !---I mean, Sir--- my papa---likes a race. Sir, your moſt obedient humble ſervant.

YOUNG PRANKS.

Madam, (*they part with great ceremony and ten- dernefs.*) [*Exit Kitty into the houfe.*

YOUNG PRANKS.

Oh, by Heavens ! ſhe's a cherubim ! a good for- tune, I dare ſay---thinks me rolling in gold. .Ah ! ſhe'll be in all the faſhionable blaze of Weymouth, and ſhou'd I ſee her, I muſt ſneak out of the way with my empty pockets.

Enter PEREGRINE.

PEREGRINE.

I was right enough---'tis Tom Pranks.

YOUNG PRANKS.

What ! my worthy Cambridge Johnian, George Peregrine ? ah ! how d'ye do ?

PEREGRINE.

Ah ! but Tom, what has brought you here ? what are you on ?

YOUNG PRANKS.

I'm on air, fire---Are you on a viſit down here ?

PEREGRINE.

Viſit ! no, at home ; I've a ſort of little lodge hard by, at which I ſhall be very happy to ſee you ; but, come, what brought you down here ? To ſee Mr. Whimmy's gardens !

YOUNG PRANKS.

Whimmy! who's he? You can't conceive what a variety of high---low---jack---and game, since the morning we parted at the Shakefpeare, you in a poft-chaife for Dover. I in a phaeton for Newmarket, juft run a horfe at Blandford---loft---beft of the fun, I'm at this moment a prifoner in the King's Bench.

PEREGRINE.

A prifoner in the King's Bench, and 122 miles from town? Why, Tom, you've fkipp'd out of bounds indeed! Come, how?

YOUNG PRANKS.

Why you may fuppofe, George, that my expences far exceeded my uncle's allowance---thought to help out by a lucky hit now and then, fo bought a blood mare, had her put in training, then entered for the plate at Blandford---a beautiful thing---the crack of the courfe---but before the meeting, a few pofitive mechanical rafcals thruft me into the King's Bench ---muft go to Blandford though, fo procured the rules, and in hopes the turf could bring me in money enough to pay my debts, off I fpank'd for Dorfetfhire, and, fpite of informers, appeared on the courfe. The opinion feemed all in favour of my mare; but, like a curfed green-horn, I withdrew her from the plate, and made a by-match to run her againft Lord Skelter's four-crout, to ride ourfelves ---but after the firft round, my infernal groom told me I carried too much weight, flung part away, came in firft; but my Lord infifting on our being again weighed, I was too light by a pound and an half, fo that though I won, I loft the race; two hundred to my Lord; in fhort, every guinea of a full

five

five hundred that an honeft methodift preacher, my landlord in the rules, raifed to equip me for the expedition.

PEREGRINE.

Ah, Tom! I thought when you and I were at Cambridge together, your fcampers to Newmarket would turn to this at laft.

YOUNG PRANKS.

Certainly it's life, my boy.---You were always a dead fag, and I was a blood. You know I never could prevail on you, even then, to make one of our toxophilite club.

PEREGRINE.

But where are you going now?

YOUNG PRANKS.

Can you tell me? Dem'me if I can tell *you*.---Sir, I was diftreffed---diftracted---I---

PEREGRINE.

Ay! but Tom, your mare,---as fhe won---

YOUNG PRANKS.

She's gone; fold her for five hundred---went to dinner, tuck'd three bottles under my girdle---hopp'd off as fteady as old time to the affembly, laugh'd at the minuets--- tol lol, (*mimicks*) adjourned to a fnug hazard party---loft every face---roll'd into the ftreet at eight in the morning---faw a carriage at the Greyhound door---pretty girl all alone ---finding it was a return chaife, ftept in without knowing whither bound---had a moft delectable chat---a lovely creature---fingle---hither we've come ---fhe's there---I'm here---fhe's an angel with a great fortune---I'm a dog without the price of a collar.

D   PEREGRINE.

PEREGRINE.

Ha! ha! ha! Well this is a moſt curious detail of your adventures. Tom you hav'n't heard, perhaps, I'm going to be married to the heireſs of the Caſtle yonder?

YOUNG PRANKS.

Indeed! this is your muzzing for a fellowſhip.

PEREGRINE.

But won't you return to the King's Bench?

YOUNG PRANKS.

No! can't do that; they'd never let me out again.

PEREGRINE.

Yes; but if you're found out here, it will be worſe: what will you do?

YOUNG PRANKS.

What will I do? Damn it, you're always putting me to the mathematics: fling by your Euclid, and you tell me what I' ſhall do.

PEREGRINE.

Ha! ha! ha! the very thing for you, Tom, ha! ha! ha!

YOUNG PRANKS.

Plague of your ſneer; what are you at?

PEREGRINE.

Read that paper.

YOUNG PRANKS.

Paper! what's this? (*reads an advertiſement which is poſted up againſt the ſign poſt.*) " A liberal offer.—A " perſon wanted to ſit dreſſed as a hermit in the her-

3   " mitage

" mitage of very capital gardens : on condition of his
" attendance for feven years, he will be entitled to
" a gratuity of two thoufand pounds, and three hun-
" dred a year for the remainder of his life.—For par-
" ticulars inquire within."—Eh! what's all this about?
Hermit !

PEREGRINE.

Tom, why fuppofe you apply for this.

YOUNG PRANKS.

Me! what I turn hermit ?—Pooh, nonfenfe ! a
high go, faith.

PEREGRINE.

Will your uncle pay your debts ?

YOUNG PRANKs.

He ! I've got a hint 'twas he threw me into prifon.—No ! never fhall I touch an ounce of his.

PEREGRINE.

A couple of thoufands---three hundred a year
for life !

YOUNG PRANKS.

Oh ! but how you'd it tell among one's friends ?
mine are all bloods, my dear.

PEREGRINE.

While you can keep pace with them in flafh and
expence : but drove into a corner by ficknefs or po-
verty, there they leave you.

YOUNG PRANKS.

Three hundred a year---

PEREGRINE.

If you think it an object, I'll anfwer for your getting the fituation.

YOUNG

YOUNG PRANKS.

What elfe can I do? for when I came into this village, I didn't know which way to turn my face; back to London I cannot go; I'll have it---two thoufand! three hundred a year! I'll have it.   Tol, lol.

PEREGRINE.

No, but ftop—can I believe that you'd continue feven years?

YOUNG PRANKS.

Seven thoufand! Be independent of uncle—drefs'd up in a gown and long beard, dam'me, I'll be a fine old bald-headed buck—befides the change of perfon, if the marfhal fhould fend conftables down here after me—the very thing!

PEREGRINE.

Stop in the houfe a few minutes and I'll aequaint Mr. Whimmy.

YOUNG PRANKS.

Do, tell him I'll be a hermit, a pilgrim. *(Sings.)*

> In pennance for paft folly,
> A Pilgrim blythe and jolly.   [*Exeunt.*
> *Young Pranks goes into the houfe.*]

SCENE

SCENE II. *A Room in the Inn.*

Enter BARLEYCORN.

BARLEYCORN.

Oh! the gentlefolks that came from Weymouth by water; they feem to have got a foufing.

Poz without.

POZ.

All your fault, Bite.

BITE *(without.)* Mine! 'twas your's, Mr. Poz.

Enter POZ *and* BITE.

POZ.

You know you wou'dn't let the fail be up.

BITE.

If it had we fhou'd have tipp'd over, been knock'd againft Durdle Door rock, as they call it.

POZ.

I know better; we fhou'd ha' fkim'd like a fwal-low—boxing about three hours in dabbling oars.

BITE.

I wifh we had dinner; I'm proud to fay I'm quite peckifh.

POZ:

Ay! you peck'd all the way at the ham and cold fowls.

BITE,

BITE.

We were so blown about—the wind sharpens one's appetite.

POZ.

I know better—we came upon a party of pleasure, and had nothing but crosses and wrangling. Keep your temper like Mr. Apathy yonder.

BITE.

Aye! because Mr. Apathy's a man of fashion, his absent insipidity is thought agreeable.

Enter APATHY *and* LADIES.

FIRST LADY.

Water excursion! horrid!

APATHY.

And this is a party of pleasure, *(yawns.)*

FIRST LADY.

Some vulgar club-room, I suppose;

BITE.

This the president's chair?

POZ.

Aye, it just suits a fat beadle.

APATHY.

So it does. Will you please to sit, Ma'am, *(hands it to First Lady.)*

FIRST LADY.

Offer me a great chair, indeed.

Enter

Enter KITTY.

KITTY.

Oh ! that dear fweet gentleman—from his having fuch fine running horfes, he muft be certainly fome great fquire. Heigh ho ! *(fits in the great chair.)*

FIRST LADY.

Pray do you know this young lady ?

BITE.

Mifs, will you take a glafs of negus ?

BARLEYCORN.

I ax pardon. Mifs, will you be kind enough to go boil the lobfters for the company ? Dang my buttons, this is letting you go to Blandford races— I'll buy riding habits and feather'd hats for you—go put on your mob-cap and white apron—there's the keys—get along.

KITTY.

I fhall, father ; don't be angry. As that charming gentleman doesn't fee me in this mean fituation, I don't care what any body elfe thinks of me ; but he's far off by this, *(afide.)* What wou'd you pleafe to have, ladies ?—Father, I hope the gentlemen haven't been long waiting. Here, Toby. I'll look to every thing myfelf, father ; don't make yourfelf uneafy. [*Exit.*

FIRST LADY.

Oh ! then, good man, that is your daughter ?

BITE.

We were fo blown about—the wind fharpens one's appetite.

POZ.

I know better—we came upon a party of plea-fure, and had nothing but croffes and wrangling. Keep your temper like Mr. Apathy yonder.

BITE.

Aye! becaufe Mr. Apathy's a man of fafhion, his abfent infipidity is thought agreeable.

Enter APATHY *and* LADIES.

FIRST LADY.

Water excurfion! horrid!

APATHY.

And this is a party of pleafure, *(yawns.)*

FIRST LADY.

Some vulgar club-room, I fuppofe;

BITE.

This the prefident's chair?

POZ.

Aye, it juft fuits a fat beadle.

APATHY.

So it does. Will you pleafe to fit, Ma'am, *(hands it to Firft Lady.)*

FIRST LADY.

Offer me a great chair, indeed.

Enter

Enter KITTY.

KITTY.

Oh! that dear fweet gentleman—from his having fuch fine running horfes, he muft be certainly fome great fquire. Heigh ho! *(fits in the great chair.)*

FIRST LADY.

Pray do you know this young lady?

BITE.

Mifs, will you take a glafs of negus?

BARLEYCORN.

I ax pardon. Mifs, will you be kind enough to go boil the lobfters for the company? Dang my buttons, this is letting you go to Blandford races— I'll buy riding habits and feather'd hats for you—go put on your mob-cap and white apron—there's the keys—get along.

KITTY.

I fhall, father; don't be angry. As that charming gentleman doesn't fee me in this mean fituation, I don't care what any body elfe thinks of me; but he's far off by this, *(afide.)* What wou'd you pleafe to have, ladies?—Father, I hope the gentlemen haven't been long waiting. Here, Toby. I'll look to every thing myfelf, father; don't make yourfelf uneafy. [*Exit.*

FIRST LADY.

Oh! then, good man, that is your daughter?

BAR-

Enter KITTY, (*in a plain drefs, with a bowl in her hand.*)

KITTY.

Did you pleafe to call? this brandy and water for you, Sir?---Oh, Lord! I fhall fink with fhame, (*afide.*)

YOUNG PRANKS.

My dear, if you pleafe to get me---Eh! why 'tis certainly fhe? could fhe have fo much deception? but I'll not diftrefs her, (*afide.*)

KITTY, (*confufed.*)

Sir, I---I---the---the waiter---fhall bring---you what---you want.

YOUNG-PRANKS.

Poor thing! I feel her confufion from my foul, (*afide*) I---do, Mifs---Ma'am---my dear---I---I---dam'me but I'm as much confufed as herfelf! I---hem!---Irang the bell.

KITTY.

Yes, Sir---you call'd---I thought you call'd---you wanted---

YOUNG PRANKS.

Yes, my dear, I wanted---that is it.---Curfe me if I know what I wanted, (*afide*). Her modefty gives me fome hope that this may have been the firft little art fhe was ever guilty of.

KITTY.

Toby! bring the gentleman the---the---Sir, you fhall have it prefently.   [*Exit with emotion.*

YOUNG PRANKS.

You moft delicate piece of artful lovelinefs!---
now is fhe the maid or daughter of the Red Lion?
the daughter fhe muft be. Oh! ho! now I fee her
wifh for the filver cup---dam'me I wifh I cou'd win
it for her. I've my jockey drefs here ready (*puts his
hand on the valife,*) and wou'd ride, but a horfe is
neceffary. This lovely impoftor---fuch a fair cheat!
old Grumps waiting to bring her to grandpappa! a
very good offer that, faith, ha! ha! ha! Oh! this
has clinch'd it. I'll turn hermit for one-and-twenty
years, if only to be near this beautiful hypocrite,

Enter SKIP.

SKIP,

Sir, I believe you are the gentleman---Mr. Peregrine's compliments, would be glad to fee you up
at my mafter's. [*Exit.*

YOUNG PRANKS.

Very well, Sir! I've a mind to ring the bell again
for another look at this charming girl---girl! true,
I'm a hermit.

" In pennance for paft folly,
" A pilgrim blythe and jolly."
[*Exit finging,*

END OF ACT I.

ACT II.

SCENE I. *Before the Inn.*

Enter from it TOBY *and* POZ.

POZ.

WELL, where is this man?

TOBY, (*looking about,*)

He's not in the road, nor he's not in the houfe, nor he's not in the ftable, nor he's not in—

POZ.

Zounds! I don't want to know where he is *not*--- where is he?

TOBY.

Here be the very mon.

POZ, (*looking out.*)

Eh! what Ham Barebones, the Methodift preacher, informer, pedlar, money-lender, broker, old-cloaths-man, in the way of my profeffion a moft choice friend; the converfation between him and I won't admit of a third perfon. (*To Toby*) Has your mafter no call for you? but you muft ftand grinning here.

TOBY.

TOBY.

Yes, Sir, I've the knives to rub, and dinner-tables to fet out; but I'll be in the way, for I know when a lawyer comes down here amongft us, he foon cuts out work for the conftable. [*Exit.*

Enter BAREBONES.

POZ.

Ah! Mafter Barebones, fo far from London, how doft do?

BAREBONES.

Lives---as much as honeft folks can do now-a-days.

POZ.

I know better, my old friend; you'll live where an honeft man will ftarve.

BAREBONES, (*canting.*)

Vhen I vas a coal-heaver, my face vas a black angel, but my inward man vas as vhite as a vhite vall that is vhite.

POZ.

Plague o'your canting to me! any bufinefs? Come, to it.

BAREBONES.

I am a tender Chriftian, and vith my money I did relieve the poor by lending it them.

POZ.

On good intereft.

BARE-

BAREBONES.

I did take care of myfelf; I did lend five hundred pounds to a young Muſter Pranks.

POZ.

What ! are you telling me this ? Wasn't it I that threw him into the King's Bench for you ?

BAREBONES.

As he received the money by a third hand, not knowing I vas the creditor, vhen he got the rules he did take lodgings in my houſe in St. George's Fields; I did advife him to run away, he did; then I did tell the Marſhal.

POZ,

But I fuppofe, as you knew where he went, you'll try to re-take him for the reward.

BAREBONES.

I'll do that thing. 'Twas to run a horfe at Bland-ford races that made him run from his bail. Don't you know him ?

POZ.

No ! when I fend a man to quod, 'tis enough for me if my bailiff knows him. Lucky for you find-ing me here ; I come down to Weymouth on buſi-nefs; as I ſhall charge my client three guineas a day for my travelling expences, I thought I might as well give my wife a little country air and a fea-dip ---left her behind, ill at Weymouth, when I came upon this water excurfion to fee Mr. Whimmy's improvements. Barebones, I'm in genteel company, fo don't feem to know me---Oh ! yonder I fee they're going into the gardens; you and I will talk over this affair.

BAREBONES.

You are encompaſſed with the wicked---I am moved by the ſpirit.

[*Exit Barebones as in ejaculation.*

POZ.

Ha! ha! ſanctified muns and rogue's heart. [*Exit.*

SCENE II. *A magnificent Garden, with Statues, Fountains, &c.*

Enter WHIMMY, (*repeating with great exultation*)

    " I build, I plant whatever I intend,
    " I rear the column, and the arch I bend,
    " I ſwell the terrace, or I ſink the grot,
    " My taſte refined"----

The company flocking in already to ſee my gardens; that tough old bully Pranks won't even pay me the compliment. I muſt have a good ſupper for him tho', or he'll do nothing but quarrel---give orders to Mrs. Maggs, my houſekeeper, about it. Oh! here ſhe is. Since I ſet her to ſhow my houſe and pictures, it has given her ſuch a conſequential ---all talk herſelf, but never liſtens to any body elſe, always dinning in my ears the grandeur of the laſt people ſhe lived with; nothing but the family of the Olmondles.

Enter

Enter Mrs. MAGGS.

WHIMMY.

Mrs. Maggs, you muſt---

MRS. MAGGS.

Well, Sir, I know that very well.

WHIMMY.

What, before I tell you! a gentleman ſups with me to-night.

MRS. MAGGS.

Well, Sir, I know a gentleman ſups with you.

WHIMMY.

Ay! you know now I tell you; and I'll have---

MRS. MAGGS.

Well, Sir, I know what you'd have.

WHIMMY.

Before I tell you! I muſt be ſure have a brill and variety of other fiſh.

MRS. MAGGS.

Well, I know you muſt have a brill, and variety of other fiſh.

WHIMMY.

Certainly you know when I tell you. Beſides all other wines, as my friend is a London ſoaker, have ſome of my oldeſt port, ſome bottled porter, and a pipe.

MRS.

MRS. MAGGS.

Well, I know you muſt have bottled porter and pipe of port.

WHIMMY.

Now you know nothing at all about it—go along.

MRS. MAGGS.

Ah! when I lived with Squire Olmondle, he never bid me go along.

WHIMMY.

Stupid wife fool!

MRS. MAGGS.

Ah! the Olmondles! that was the genteel family that knew how to treat a houſekeeper like a gentlewoman.

WHIMMY.

Damn the Olmondles! I deteſt the very name; it grates my ear like cutting of cork—a teaſing ninny! you know all, won't let any body elſe know any thing, and after all know nothing at all. Mrs. Maggs, ſtep and bring me word.

MRS. MAGGS.

Certainly, Sir, I'll bring you word---(*going.*)

WHIMMY.

Of what now? See if the young man, the hermit that I hir'd---

MRS. MAGGS.

Well, Sir, I know that.

. F

WHIMMY,

Ay! you know that and this—and after that, Mrs. Maggs, you muft—

MRS. MAGGS.

Well, Sir, I will, you may depend upon it. [*Exit.*

WHIMMY.

Now what will fhe! never knew one of your profefs'd, notable, clever women worth a penny in a houfe, but to fay all and do nothing. Where's my—Oh! Tully, my Irifh gard'ner?

Enter TULLY.

Tully, have you placed my new hermit yet at his poft?

TULLY.

Ay! faith, and he ftarted for the poft; for as I led him thro' the paddock yonder, up he jumps upon a little horfe, and away he fcampered as if the devil was before him, round the fifh-pond.

WHIMMY.

My hermit galloping round a fifh-pond! Tully, to-morrow you may go with the other fervants to Wool Fair, but to-day you muft brufh up all your eloquence for your poft of Ciceroni to defcribe the attic urbanity of my Englifh Tufculum here. But mind, Tully, I command you not to take a penny from one of the company.

TULLY.

A penny! not I, Sir: but mayn't I take half-a-crown if they offer it?

WHIMMY.

No. Gentlemen fuffering the public to pay their fervants wages, and turning their own houfes into a Sadlers Wells and a Royal Grove, is mean. I never paid for feeing pictures in palaces and grape vines in gardens, that I didn't blufh for the difgrace thrown upon the dignity of the owner. Is the water party come that ftopt at the Red Lion?

TULLY.

Yes, Sir. Mrs. Maggs is now fhowing them the houfe. Ah! fhe told them, that the picture of Mary Magdalen was Mrs. Molly Olmondle,

WHIMMY.

A moft horrid—

TULLY.

Sir, don't fret about that woman; you know in the fhowing way I'll bring up your credit with a wet finger; Mrs. Maggs will infift that this is a py-ramid—now pray, Sir, isn't it an *obfticle?* I muft go and put on my Wednefday's fine fuit of cloaths that you gave me to fhow the gardens in.—What country fellow's that ftalking about the walks—only I'm in a hurry to drefs myfelf, or by my foul I'd knock his head againft the gateway.

WHIMMY.

Stop, Tully, pray remember the names and cha-racters of the feveral antiques.

TULLY.

I'll tell 'em of your anticks. [*Exit.*

WHIMMY.

WHIMMY.

Obſticle! my anticks! very ignorant this ſaid Maſter Tully; I muſt watch how you go on with your deſcription.—Poor Peregrine thinks he marries my daughter to-morrow, I've ſcarce the heart to kill him with the diſappointment.—I ſhou'd like to come at the people's real opinion of my gardens and improvements.

Enter a WAGGONER, (*whiſtling and ſtaring about.*)

WHIMMY.

Were you deſired to walk in here?

WAGGONER.

Noa! 'twas my own fancy.

WHIMMY.

Why then it's my own fancy that you walk out again.　-

WAGGONER.

Ah! if I thought I cou'dn't do that I ſhou'dn't have comd in, I can tell thee.

WHIMMY.

What! keep your diſtance.

WAGGONER.

I wool; becauſe, at the ſame time, you keep your's—　　　　　　　　(*A laughing without.*)

WHIMMY.

Oh! the company. I wiſh to hear how Mr. Tully performs his office of orator. If I could mix amongſt them without being known—this clodpate's hat, wig, and frock, may do it—you've no objection to a draught of ſtrong beer and a ſlice of beef?

WAG-

WAGGONER.

Noa !

WHIMMY.

(*Mimicking.*)   Noa ! then come with me.

WAGGONER.

I wool.

WHIMMY, (*turns to look at him.*)
Doo ! (*mimicking.*)

WAGGONER.

Yez,   [*Exeunt.*

Enter TULLY, *in a suit of tarnished laced cloaths and a bag wig, with a small white rod in his hand, followed by* BITE, POZ, APATHY, BAREBONES, *and* LADIES.

TULLY.

Hem ! my Lady, this is counted the finest place in all Ireland—England I mean.

BAREBONES.

Pagan wanity !

SECOND LADY.

What noife is this under ground ?

TULLY.

My Lady, its the fuccedaneous river of black Tartary ; it creeps over fticks and ftones like an eel, hops like a trout, and then jumps like a falmon up the rocks yonder ; then it fails away fo gay into the fea like a maiden ray.

BARE-

BAREBONES.

(*Apart to Poz.*) I've fpoken with the poft-chaife boy that did drive a gemman and the girl of the alehoufe to the village here, and by the defcription it's young Mr. Pranks, the man ve vants.

POZ.

(*Apart.*) The parifh conftable is the waiter at the Red Lion, engage him to arreft—hem !

Enter WHIMMY *in a waggoner's frock, &c.*

WHIMMY.

I don't think they can know me—now I fhall hear how my gard'ner performs his office, (*afide.*)

BITE.

What figure call you this ? (*points to a ftatue.*)

TULLY.

Ay ! you're a nice figure to come thruft your nofe into the company of ladies and gentlemen, (*to Whimmy.*)

BITE.

No ! I mean this.

TULLY.

That's Venus, the goddefs of med'cine—a pretty employment I've got to throw away my roratory and knowledge to divart fuch dirty blackguards as you. (*to Whimmy*)—this is—

WHIMMY.

Apollo of Belvidere, (*apart.*)

TULLY.

TULLY.

Ay! that's Poll the bell-weather, that run after Daphne, and was kick'd out of heaven by Jove, (I'll be free) and so turn'd cow-boy to—

WHIMMY

Shepherd to king Admetus, (*apart.*)

TULLY.

Ay! they'll all meet us; but who bid you put in your prate?

FIRST LADY.

Heavens! who is that?

TULLY.

That is—that is, (*confused*)—that is, my Lady—I don't know what it is myself, (*aside*)—Why, your Honour, it's not a watch-box, nor it's not a wheel-barrow, nor it's not a—

WHIMMY.

(*Whispering.*) Minerva—Pallas.

TULLY.

It's not a palace, or a cake-house—I wish you'd hold your gab—you made me say it was a watch-box just now—why it's marvle, it's all made of marvle.

SECOND LADY.

But the lady marvles who 'twas made for.

TULLY.

Oh! 'twas made for my master; he bought it from the stone-man.

3

POZ.

Is it like ?---

TULLY.

I'm glad you like it.

FIRST LADY.

This I ſuppoſe is—

TULLY.

Not at all, my Lady, 'tis, 'tis—

WHIMMY.

(*Apart.*)   Saturn eating his child—

TULLY.

Yes, Ma'am, 'tis the child eating citron—will you hold your prate, (*to Whimmy*)—this, gentlemen and ladies, is—

BAREBONES.

Idolatry !

TULLY.

What is it ? Pooh ! Now had not you beſt all teach me inſtead of I larning you ! You ſee, your Honour, he has a flute in his mouth.

WHIMMY.

Such a damn'd Iriſh plough-ploy !

TULLY.

Ay ! " The Iriſh plough-boy that whiſtled o'er " the lea," that's the man.

POZ.

POZ.

Curs'd ftout fellow this, Who is he?

WHIMMY.

(*Apart.*)   Hercules of Farnefe.

TULLY.

It's not bare knees, but big knees and big legs,
—that's the tir'd paver refting himfelf on his ftone
paving-ftick.

WHIMMY.

Oh heavens! I've fent to Italy for a fine purpofe,
(*afide.*)

TULLY.

But I'm talking here by word of mouth, when I
might fay it all in reading, as I have it by heart
from my defcribing-book---now I defire you'll hold
your tongues, for if you talk, you'll put me out;
pleafe your Honour, hem! (*takes out a book and
looks at it*) " Thefe gar"---Oh! now I go on velvet; Thefe gardens, which are now the admiration
of the larn'd and curifh, were once a barren flat,
like Salifbury Plain, till Mr. Humphry Freak
Whimmy, Efq. gave forty thoufand pounds for the
ould caftle and lands, turn'd the courfe of the river
through them, and with Roman tafte and Britifh
magnificence---

APATHY.

(*Advancing.*)   Pray, friend, (*looking at his watch*)
what o'clock is it?

G

TULLY, *(confused.)*

Roman---half an hour after one---two---Roman---two---Roman---breeches---hem !---breeches--Britiſh magnificence---the river---in the ould caſtle---ran !---round the lands. The curiſh---of Saliſbury Plain. The devil's in this man, and his what o'clock is it ? He's put me all out--ſo I muſt--my deſcribing book. *(Takes out his book, wets his thumb, and turns over the leaves haſtily, and vex'd.)* Bri-tiſh mag-ni-fi-ci---Oh! here it is, *(Looking and reading.)* Having firſt travell'd to ſee the ancient beauties of Italy, I-I-taly---I---*(Looks again.)* Italy, *(Puts the book behind his back.)* and ſelected with claſſical---Ah! ah! claſſical---Ah! damnation ! *(Thruſts the book into his pocket.)* Theſe gardens which are now the admiration of the larned and curiſh, were once a barren flat like Saliſbury Plain, till Mr. Humphrey Freak------

APATHY.

Oh! my----Pray, my friend, does Mr. Freak take ſnuff ?

TULLY.

Yes, blackguard---till Humphrey Freak Whimmy, Eſquire----Humphrey, Eſquire---Saliſbury Street---pooh !----the Plain----larned and curiſh---river upon the ould caſtle—land turned---aboat---about---

FIRST LADY.

Why the orator's in a hobble.

TULLY.

Orator Hobble---oh ! the devil take---I was ſailing on like a young ſwan, till this fellow comes with his ſnuff-box. *(Very quick.)* Theſe gardens, which are now the admiration of the larn'd and curiſh, were

were once a barren flat like Salifbury Plain, *(drops the book, ftoops to pick it up)* till Humphrey Freak Whimmy, Efquire, gave forty thoufand pounds for the ould caftle, *(Apathy picks it up)* and lands round it. *(Looks at Apathy.)*

APATHY, *(opens and reads.)*

Turning to the left you wind through a moft delicious fhrubbery.

TULLY, *(confufed.)*

Humphrey Freak---a barren flat. My mafter's a flat.

APATHY.

You reach the labyrinth. *(Reading.)*

TULLY,

Like Salifbury Plain.

APATHY.

So intricate that you're puzzled to get out. *(Reading.)*

TULLY.

I'm puzzled to get out---I'm out---Humphrey Whimmy---

WHIMMY.

Damn'd blockhead!

TULLY.

Is a damn'd blockhead.

ALL.

Ha! ha! ha!

TULLY.

TULLY.

Well, ladies and gentlemen, I don't wonder at your laughing at my mafter's nonfenfe in laying out fo much money on the balderdafh you fee round about you here. But, ladies and gentlemen, though my mafter's a fool, you'll remember my trouble, I hope. (*Stretching out his hand.*)

WHIMMY.

Not a farthing. (*Apart to him.*)

TULLY.

Why a didn't expeft any thing from fuch an ill-looking beggarly whelp as you. Will you walk out of the grounds, if you plaife, Sir? The next thing you're to fee is-----

WHIMMY.

An aviary and pheafantry.

TULLY.

Yes, my mafter's knavery and pleafantry. Then there is King Pluto's Tartary---then my mafter's Ely-fian Fields---then my mafter's hanging wood, where my mafter will hang himfelf, and then the hermitage.

WHIMMY.

If the new hermit's not ready, he'll difgrace me as much as my worthy gard'ner has done. (*Going.*) I muft be fure.---

TULLY.

Oh! ftop---you and your farthing. Pretty manners to walk out before the gentlemen and ladies, that know how to pay their money.

BARE-

BAREBONES.

The fpirit doth whifper, " Ham Barebones arife,
" and fpeak the word to thy deluded brethren."---
Down, accurfed Dagon. (*Puſhes down a ſtatue and
ſtands upon the pedeſtal.*)

TULLY.

Why, then I fuppofe you think yourfelf a fine
Roman buſt. The devil's in your aſſurance to cock
yourfelf up there ! If you plaife, you'll walk down.

BAREBONES.

Brethren, I vas a coal-heaver, but on the ſtony
cage where I now ſtand, I have brought you fome
bifcuits, baked in the oven of charity, carefully con-
farved for the chickens of the church, and the fweet
fwallows of-----
(*A ſudden noiſe without of falling water.*)

TULLY.

Oh ! the devil !---If what o'clock hasn't pull'd up
a fluice. Half the garden will be overflowed ; and
we ſhall have the carp and tench dancing among the
daifes. [*Exeunt haſtily ſeveral ways.*

SCENE II. *Another part of the Gardens, with the
view of the Outſide of an Hermitage.*

Enter KITTY BARLEYCORN.

KITTY.

The race is over, and I not fee it. Since this
dear gentleman is obligated to take a hermit's place,
. he

he can't be angry at my playing off the fine lady upon him-----In there he sits.

(*Points at the hermitage.*)

Enter at the side YOUNG PRANKS *in a loose coat, with a silver cup.*

YOUNG PRANKS.

Huzza, my girl! the day is your's.

KITTY.

The gracious!—

YOUNG PRANKS.

Tully left me in the hermitage---flipt out again---flung off my gown, beard, and girdle---had my jockey-drefs that I rode in at Blandford ready under it---the poney I found younder; had firft try'd it though---fpank up the hill---four poor jades ready to ftart---a village race---horfe, mare, colt, or filly---I was enter'd---rode myfelf---won. Huzza the glorious prize is your's. (*Gives her the cup.*)

KITTY.

What a wild gentleman! Sir, don't think little of me for the fib I told you this morning.

YOUNG PRANKS.

No, my fweeteft, when a man's heart is fet in a flame by fuch a charming girl as you, it isn't a cup of tea that can extinguifh it.

KITTY.

Wou'd you have a cup of tea, Sir?---la! Sir, your hav'n't din'd.

YOUNG PRANKS.

Oh ! yes, my dear, I did---yefterday. (*Afide.*)

KITTY.

It's Mr. Whimmy's way not to allow the hermit any dinner on the day when the company's expeded: but, ecod, you fhan't faft while my father's houfe affords a dinner. (*Afide.*)---But, what did you come down here and turn hermit for ?

YOUNG PRANKS.

For love of you, my dear---dying for you thefe five years.

KITTY.

Sure !

YOUNG PRANKS.

Never faw you before this morning. (*Afide.*)----- (*Looking out.*) The very Lady I danc'd with at Bland- ford affembly !---My love, a gentleman comes yon- der with whom I muft talk politics. (*Kiffes her.*)

KITTY.

The deuce is in you for a hermit.   [*Exit.*

Enter DIAN.

DIAN.

I---I wifh my father, with his other changes of humour, wou'd give up this fancy of refigning the houfe thus to ftrangers; people, one don't know who, every Wednefday here come ftamping and ftaring about---even my dreffing-room is not my own.

YOUNG

YOUNG PRANKS.

My charming angel, to meet you here!

DIAN.

Blefs me, Sir, you!---I hope you're very well, Sir?

YOUNG PRANKS,

On a vifit here?

DIAN.

No, Sir, this is my father's houfe.

YOUNG PRANKS.

Her father's houfe!---Oh! here may be another crufty old grumps. And hem! my dear, you love riding on a pillion, like Queen Elizabeth going in ftate.

DIAN.

Sir!

YOUNG PRANKS.

I mean---your parlour cuftomers like to drink out of filyer.

DIAN.

Parlour cuftomers!---But the unexpected honour of feeing you here!

YOUNG PRANKS.

Merely for admiffion to you, my angel; I've hired as your father's hermit---dying for you ever fince we parted---a fine creature---but demme, if I ever thought of you fince. (*Afide.*)

DIAN.

DIAN.

I thought you then a rattler, and find I was right, ---but don't teafe me now with nonfenfe, for I'm really diftrefs'd.

YOUNG PRANKS.

Eh! Peregrine's intended, diftrefs'd! eh!---how? tell me---you may. Why, my dear Ma'am, I'm--- you don't know, perhaps, that I'm your Peregrine's moft intimate friend.

DIAN.

Was it, indeed, you I faw juft now arm-in-arm with him?---Oh! then you don't know, perhaps, that my father, after giving his fanction to the addreffes of a young gentleman in the neighbourhood, now fuddenly changes his mind, and infifts upon my marrying the nephew of fome old friend of his.--- Yonder's Peregrine, (*looking out*) he hasn't yet heard this unlucky news. 　　　　　　[*Exit haftily.*

Young Pranks, (*whiftles.*)

My friend, Peregrine's intended fpofa; I had hopes, that if he got this lady and her fortune, he might tip me a thoufand pounds, without a feven year's imprifonment in the old gentleman's hermitage; but borrowing money is throwing water upon the warm heart of friendfhip. (*Laughing without.*) 'Sdeath, the company!-----I muft now earn my annuity.-----Heh! is that Kitty gliding through the bufhes?---a moft dear dangerous little Barleycorn this. Marriage is all out of fight, and, without it, to take all a fimple young girl's innocence may beftow, would be, indeed, giving life in my breaft to the worm that never dies. 　　　[*Goes into the Hermitage.*

H 　　　　　　　　　　　SCENE

SCENE III. *The Hermitage.*

Enter KITTY, *with meat and drink for* YOUNG PRANKS, *and knocks at the door.*

KITTY, *(finging.)*

" Fair Ellinor came to Lord Thomas's bow'r,
" And pull'd fo hard at the ring,"—

Are you within, Mr. Hermit?

Enter MRS. MAGGS.

MRS. MAGGS.

This poor hermit mus'n't fit here, and have no dinner. My mafter has got fo crufty with me of late, that I'm quite weary of looking after other people's concerns; and as our young lady's to be married to-morrow, this will be no place for me. If I cou'd get a man to my mind, I'd keep houfe for myfelf, and this handfome fellow is juft to my liking.------ Befides, my conceited fon, Natty Maggs, is foon out of his time; he fhall have a father to thrafh him, when he gets faucy to me.

KITTY.

The hermit's Wednefday allowance is roots and cold water, but---

" None fo ready as Lord Thomas,
" To let fair Ellinor in."

MRS. MAGGS.

What are you doing here, Kitty Barleycorn?

KITTY.

KITTY.

O Lord! Mrs. Maggs the houfekeeper! Ma'am,
I was going---

MRS. MAGGS.

I know you was going. Child, do you know the
danger of a young woman like you, reforting to this
lonely place, where this new-come hermit fits with
his books, and his fkull, and his crofs bones? Do
you know, Kitty, that this hermit may be a ram-
fcallion?

KITTY.

Yes, Ma'am---to be fure, Ma'am---Thank ye,
Ma'am---

MRS. MAGGS.

What have you got there?

KITTY.

A little eatables and a little drinkables.

MRS. MAGGS.

For this Mr. Tom?

KITTY.

Yes, Ma'am. (*Curtfies.*)

MRS. MAGGS.

Then you were now going to fee him?

KITTY.

Yes, Ma'am. (*Curtfies.*)

MRS. MAGGS.

And you'd have heard fome love nonfenf: from
him?

H 2

KITTY.

KITTY.

Yes, Ma'am. (*Curtſies.*)

MRS. MAGGS.

And you think me very impertinent for interrupting you?

KITTY.

Yes, Ma'am. (*Curtſies.*)

MRS. MAGGS.

Child, take example from me---Do you think I'd ſit there alone, to eat and drink with any ſtrange hermit?

KITTY.

Yes, Ma'am. (*Curtſies.*)

Enter JOHN, *with a Tray of covered Diſhes.*

JOHN.

Mrs. Maggs, here, I've brought the dinner.

MRS. MAGGS.

What dinner? --Go along! (*Apart, confuſed.*)

JOHN.

Why, the roaſt fowl for you and the hermit, as you ordered me.   [*Exit.*

KITTY, (*mimicking.*)

Child, do you know the danger of a young woman, like you, going into this lonely place? Do you know, Mrs. Maggs, that this hermit may be a ramſcallion?---Ha! ha! ha!   [*Exit:*

2

TULLY.

TULLY, (*without.*)

Now, if you plaife, your honour, don't walk
upon the grafs beds.

MRS. MAGGS.

Oh ! [*Steals off.*

SCENE IV. *Infide of an Hermitage.* Young Pranks
*difcovered in his Hermit's Drefs at a Table, with
lamp, fkull, bones, large book, and jockey whip.*

YOUNG PRANKS.

A hermit fhou'd have been my laft trade. Tol
de rol lol. How dev'lifh well Slingfby kick'd the
tamborine. (*Holds up a wooden trencher and kicks at it.*)
Zounds! (*Runs fuddenly and feats himfelf at a table.*)
Eh! Nobody!---I wifh that gander, Tully, wou'd
bring his flock of ftaring geefe, till I get down again
to play with my little lamb at the Red Lion. Old
Whimmy on the other days, it feems, ftints me to a
bottle. Dam'me, what's two bottles to me? how
many have I won, by jumping over the table at Med-
ley's? By'r leave pair and his nob. (*Puts the fkull
and bones by, is going to jump, but fits down fuddenly.*)

Enter TULLY, BITE, *and* LADIES.

TULLY.

The hermitage, plaife your honour.

FIRST LADY.

Is this your anchorite !

TULLY.

TULLY.

My Lady, I didn't hear he was an anchor-fmith.
He's old Father Anthony.

YOUNG PRANKS, (*repeating in a tremulous tone*)

Here I may fit and rightly tell
Of all the ftars that Heaven doth fhew
And all the herbs that fip the dew,
Till old experience—

TULLY.

Aye! what fignifies your old experience, man,
with your beard acrofs your forehead? What the
devil have you been about with your indecency?---
Now, if you can but fit quiet, Tom, juft while I explain you. (*Apart.*)

YOUNG PRANKS.

Tom!---I'll break your head. (*Apart.*)

TULLY.

Will you? arrah, man, I'll break your two heads,
plaife your honours. (*Apart.*)

Enter WHIMMY, (*in the Carter's Drefs---Tully ftares
at him.*)

WHIMMY.

My farcophagus defaced,---my Hercules thrown
down,---my labyrinth overflown! Now, but let's
hear how Tully and my new galloping hermit go on.
(*Afide.*)

TULLY.

Gentlemen and ladies, this is a hermit. Here he
lives, and never ftirs out of this lonefome grotto.—
Hide your boots, you devil, you. (*To Y. Pranks.*

WHIMMY.

WHIMMY.

What! not taken off his boots?

TULLY.

What's that to you?---you've come in here too. Here he always fits at his prayers, all alone by himfelf, and nobody with him, and never fees a human foul.

YOUNG PRANKS.

Tedious fool!---I'll quicken him tho' with a touch of the rippers.

TULLY.

He's fo meek and quiet. (*Y. Pranks fpurs him, he jumps up.*) Oh! (*Alights on Whimmy's toes.*) He eats nothing but herbs.

WHIMMY.

And wild berries. (*Apart to Tully.*)

TULLY.

And goofeberries! What, you will be putting in your jabber. Lives on roots and fruits.

BITE, (*uncovers a tray.*)

Nice roaft fowl, faith!

TULLY.

Man, what bewitch'd you to fpoil my defcriptions? (*Apart to Y. Pranks.*) and drinks of the pure---

WHIMMY, (*apart.*)

------Purling rill.

TULLY.

TULLY.

He doesn't drink purl and gill.   The hermit drinks
nothing but---

WHIMMY.

(*Apart.*)   Mere element.

TULLY.

A mere elephant!

WHIMMY.

(*Apart.*)   The limpid brook.

TULLY.

I'll make you a limping rook, if you don't hold
your---He drinks nothing but---

WHIMMY.

(*Apart.*)   Water.

TULLY.

Aye! this hermit drinks nothing but clear rock
water.

BITE.

I'm proud to fay, this is (*takes up a bottle and drinks*)
dev'lifh good wine.

TULLY.

Wine and roaft chicken! why you did it on purpofe. (*Apart.*)

YOUNG PRANKS.

I wifh, whoever left them, had told me.

TULLY.

Tho' he's a clean, well-behaved old man.

YOUNG PRANKS.

Say gentleman, you rafcal. (*Apart.*)

TULLY.

Oh! be aify. An't you an old faint? (*Apart.*)

WHIMMY.

Thefe two villains muttering and quarrelling!
(*Afide.*)

TULLY.

He neither ufes napkins, nor plates, nor knives,
nor forks. All his houfehold furniture is in the
empty trunk of that hollow tree. That's his cup-
board; and there he keeps his wooden difh and his
little pitcher.

BITE.

Ah! well let's---(*Goes towards it.*)

TULLY.

There! you fee his bed is the mofs, and the herbs
and the innocent fimplicities of the earth. Go, you!
(*Pufhes Whimmy, who falls on the leaves.*)

KITTY.

Ah! (*Squalls out and difcovers herfelf under them.*)

FIRST LADY.

So! is this the hermit's fimplicity?

BITE.

And this, I am proud to fay, is his little pitcher.
(*Pulling Mrs. Maggs out of the tree—The company laugh.*)

YOUNG PRANKS, (*afide.*)

A fmart dinner---a pair of women! and I fitting
like a grave owl!

.I   *Enter*

Enter BARLEYCORN.

BARLEYCORN.

I've follow'd you, dang my buttons !---So you've com'd up here after this new hermit.

KITTY.

O father! you're the cruel step-mother. *(Barleycorn takes her off.)*

BITE.

Well, this is---

MRS. MAGGS.

Yes, Sir, I know it is as you say. I have my reasons, as Mr. Oldmondle says.

[*Curtsies round and exit.*

TULLY.

Arrah! Tom, is this like a hermit, to have Kitty and Mrs. Maggs? What do you stand shaking your fist at ? *(To Whimmy, who is threatening.)*

Enter APATHY.

APATHY.

Mr.---what's it, has a pretty looking poney in the paddock yonder; but I'd run my brute against it for fifty pounds.

YOUNG PRANKS.

Done, damme! and I'll ride myself. *(Suddenly flings off his hermit's gown, and appears in a compleat jockey dress.)* Zounds! I forgot---but since it is so, hey !---we start !---the way---knees tight---toes in---
                                                        spur

fpur out---carpet ground----flow gallop----crack----
take the lead---tough at bottom, t'other horfes wind
rakes hot----flack girt----want a fob----down ears----
whifk tail---up nofe like a pig---rattle whip---give
a-loofe---pufh for it, hey ! all to fortune, the way,
the way.   [*Exit running, and cracking his whip.*

TULLY.

Holloa! ftop, Tom; come back till I explain you
out !   [*Exeunt all but Whimmy.*

Enter PEREGRINE.

PEREGRINE.

Sir, here's—

WHIMMY, *(in a rage.)*

Sir, cou'dn't you find any man in England to
make a jeft of but me? How dare you, Sir, intro-
duce fuch a rafcal as that ? He a hermit !

PEREGRINE.

Sir, I'm very forry.

WHIMMY.

I lay out forty thoufand pounds, and then fuch a
fcoundrel to get me laugh'd at by the world ! but,
you marry no daughter of mine. A good excufe
to quarrel and put Pranks's advice into practice.
(*Afide.*) You did collect fome valuable things to be
fure, but your tafte's not confirm'd. You fhall travel again; make another feven year's tour; and, by
Heavens ! not till you return will I give you my
daughter.

I 2   PERE-

PEREGRINE.

Sir! fure you can't have the cruelty—Sir, only think.

WHIMMY.

I'm determin'd, won't hear a word.

[*Exit haftily.*

PEREGRINE.

But, Sir!

[*Exit following.*

END OF ACT THE SECOND.

ACT

ACT III.

SCENE I. *The Gardens.*

Enter OLD PRANKS.

OLD PRANKS.

TO confider on the plaguy news this puppy, my 'prentice, has brought me; he too gaping at Whimmy's raree fhow.---Natty Mags. (*Calling.*)

Enter MAGGS.

MAGGS.

(*Looking about.*) Beats Kenfington hollow!—make a fmart Vauxhall!---wants an orchefter---cafkade---a handfome box to eat cuftards.

OLD PRANKS.

The Marfhal of the King's Bench---

MAGGS.

Yes, Sir, as you defired, he gave your nephew, young Mr. Tom, the rules; but he's run away. The Marfhal's beft refpects, Sir, has got information he's down in thefe parts; a man's come after him; but he'd know if you'd have him catch'd and cag'd up again.

OLD PRANKS.

A mad dog; but like me

3

MAGGS.

MAGGS.

Yes, Sir, he's a fad rafcal.

OLD PRANKS.

What !—after all I have done for him—ingratitude is worfe than—

MAGGS.

A face without cheek whifkers.

OLD PRANKS.

Whifkers !

MAGGS.

Sir, I was only faying—by the defcription, Mr. Tom rattled off from Greyhound door at Blandford for Weymouth with a pretty girl in a poft-chaife.

OLD PRANKS.

Weymouth ! I'll have him—Step you and fetch my horfe up from the inn, firrah ! Stop, I'll go my-felf.   [*Exit.*

MAGGS.

Fetch his horfe, firrah ! As Kit Cateaton fays, the time's out for firrahs and fcoundrels—cracks over the fconce with canes—I'm not an apprentice now, to breakfaft on cold fcrag of mutton and fmall beer—retiring from table after dinner with one glafs of wine ; I'm not an apprentice now. I'll no more pu-nifh my half ounce at the playhoufe, than 'fraid to cry up, or cut down the new piece over a pint and an oyfter, but thank the footman for letting me in, and fneaking foftly up ftairs with my fhoes in my hand, and my hat in my pocket, to my flock bed in the attic.—Your authority over me is out, and I'll let you know it too, old Bounce.——I'll let him and every body know that I am out of my time.—

Nobody's

Nobody's boy ; but my own man---and dem'me I'll
fet up for myfelf. Eh ! hey !---

Enter KITTY.

KITTY.

For the foul of me I can't bide at home while this
delightful Mr. Tom the hermit is here.

MAGGS.

One of the family ! Servant, Ma'am, (*refpectfully*)
my dear, when in town, my mode to fetch a rural
faunter, crofs Holborn before breakfaft to Bagnigge
Wells, cull the newfpapers, give a twiggle on the
organ, and take a tiff of rum and milk. Shall I
thank your pretty good nature ?

KITTY.

Sir, if I had you down at our houfe, we keep the
Red Lion.

MAGGS.

Red Lion !—How d'ye do, girl ! (*familiarly impudent*) My dear, my late mafter, Mr. Pranks of Lombard-ftreet, a friend of Mr. Whimmy's, they've
agreed that young Mr. Tom Pranks—

KITTY.

La ! I heard Mr. Peregrine call my hermit by
fome'at like that name.

MAGGS.

I fuppofe every body knows he's to marry the
lady of this houfe.

KITTY.

No, Sir, it's the young lady of our houfe he's to
marry ; but I don't fet up for a lady either ; though
                                                    when

when dreſſed like, ſooth, all the folks here allows that
ſomebody would make a good ſort of a lady.   Aye !
all except Mrs. Maggs ;---but ſhe's jealous and
envious.

MAGGS.

Mrs. Maggs ! who's ſhe, pray ?

KITTY.

The 'ſquire's houſekeeper.

MAGGS.

Oh ! the devil ! true, my very honoured mother, her laſt letter, which I never anſwered, ſaid,
that ſhe was coming to live with ſome old rich Eaſt
India Quiz in this very part of the country, (aſide.)
She'll claim me as her ſon ; but I'd ſooner be found
playing at ſkettles at the Devil and Bag o'-nails.—
Oh, zounds ! yon is indeed my very mamma (looking out.)—She'll be for calling me her ſon, and her
dear boy Natty.   But dem'me, as Kit Cateaton ſays,
I'm juſt out of my time ; nobody's boy, but my own
man.   Eh ! hey !   [Exit.

KITTY.

Mr. Tom really a gentleman after all ? going to
be married to Miſs Dian ?---Ah ! that's becauſe ſhe
has fortin.----I ſhall break my heart.

Enter YOUNG PRANKS.

YOUNG PRANKS.

Ah ! my cherub---

KITTY.

Ay, Sir, now that you're going to get this great
fortin by marrying---

YOUNG PRANKS.

Marrying who! Mrs. Maggs?

KITTY.

(*Afide.*) Then he hasn't yet heard---and you'd really wed poor humble I?

YOUNG PRANKS.

Wed! Eh! Why, my love, I---I---love you to be fure, and---we'll walk and talk together, and when tired we'll fit and reft ourfelves in the hermitage, my love. Tol de rol lol, I love you fo, oh! my divine creature!---Diftraction!---Rofe buds!---Sun beams---and pretty birds! Come; but fuch innocence.---I'm in a humour now---I'll not venture into the hermitage, honour and humanity forbid it. (*Afide.*)

KITTY.

Sir, fince you're fo good as to think of a poor girl like me, you fha'n't demean yourfelf for want of being informed that you *may* have Mifs Dian and all her wealth.

YOUNG PRANKS.

I have Mifs Dian?

KITTY.

Yes, Sir, it's agreed upon.

YOUNG PRANKS:

By whom?

KITTY.

Mifs's papa and the old gentleman---Mr.---Mr.---Lud now I've forgot the name again.

K

YOUNG PRANKS.

(*Aſide.*) Can't be my uncle?---Was it---but drop
my name---may get about; and if the knabbers
ſhou'd follow me---no, no, it can't be me.---How-
ever, her intention is charming.---Kitty kiſs me,
you're a lovely—a good girl—and for your diſ-
intereſted generoſity in revealing a circumſtance that
you ſuppoſed might rob you of me; for I will be
vain enough to think you're—a—little—partial—towards—a certain ordinary fellow, (*fondling.*)—I owe
you eternal gratitude.

KITTY.

(*Sprightly.*) Oh, then you are—but my joy that
you're not to have a lady and a fortune is very ill-na-
tured of me. Don't you think ſo?

YOUNG PRANKS.

Oh! you ſweet—*(kiſſes her hand.)*

Enter BARLEYCORN.

BARLEYCORN.

Dang my buttons, go home and ſweeten the punch,
and ſqueeze the lemons.—Come and handſell your ſilver
cup; you're an honeſt lad, I muſt ſay; but if you
want any chat with my daughter, you muſt come to
my houſe for it, good Maſter Hermit.

[*Exit with Kitty.*

YOUNG PRANKS.

Well, if a publican will keep the ſign of an angel,
there a ſaint may take his bottle, *(ſings)*

" In pennance for paſt folly,
" A pilgrim blythe and jolly." [*Exit.*

SCENE

SCENE II. *Before* BARLEYCORN'S.

Enter KITTY (*in high spirits*) *and* BARLEYCORN.

BARLEYCORN.

Come, now do, child, mind the bufinefs.

KITTY.

Oh! I'm fo happy!—I've yet fome hopes that this dear—Father, though he is a hermit, he is a gentleman too.

BARLEYCORN.

Well, I'd be a gentleman if I'd nothing elfe to do.

KITTY.

I forgot my finging, I don't know how long, fince I've feen this fweet fellow, (*finging*)

" A young gentleman fhe faw."

Enter TOBY *and* JOHN GRUM *from the houfe.*

TOBY.

(*Singing.*) " Who belonged to the law."—Meafter, I'm now conftable.—Mifs Kitty, you like bachelors of every ftation.

KITTY.

Dearly!

BARLEYCORN.

Do you? it's that new come Mr. Tom has brought you to this; fo if he does marry you, let him keep you to himfelf an he can.

K 2

KITTY.

(*Sings.*) " Being at a noble wedding,

TOBY.

(*Sings.*) " In the famous town of Reading." (*ringing within.*)

BARLEYCORN.

Od dang you both, am I to be rhim'd and ballad fung, and the bufinefs of my houfe all—Will you go?

KITTY.

(*Sings.*) " If fhe's rich you'll rife to fame."

TOBY.

(*Sings.*) " If fhe's poor you are the fame." (*ringing within.*)

BARLEYCORN.

Will you go?

KITTY.

(*Sings.*) " She was left by a good grannum."

TOBY.

(*Sings.*) " Wed me, Sir, or elfe I'll fight you."

BARLEYCORN.

You'll fight me? Dang my buttons I'll fight you, and knock you to the devil, you idle rafcal; I'll fing and ballad you, (*beats him*) and you, you baggage!

KITTY.

Fathe., I believe you're uncle to the Babes in the wood.

TOBY.

You're the ould barbarous Blackamore.

BARLEY-

BARLEYCORN.

I'll (*makes a blow at Toby*)—Get in you jade, (*puts her in, and exit.*)

TOBY.

Oh! Jahn Grum, here be the mon that sent for us.

Enter BAREBONES.

BAREBONES.

According to Lawyer Poz's advice, I'll have young Mufter Pranks apprehended.—You be's a finner and a publican.

TOBY.

I'm no finner, and only farvant to the publican. Eh Jahn, I'm a bit'n a parifh conftable though, 'twas faid you wanted to attach fom'en, wa'n't it Jahn?

JOHN.

Hum!

BAREBONES.

I does. Seize him; he run'd out of prifon, Thomas Pranks is the man.

TOBY.

Oh! Thomas Pranks's man.

BAREBONES.

I thought him a farvant of grace.

TOBY.

Oh, he thought him a farvant out of place, d'ye fee, Jahn.

JOHN.

Hum!

BARE-

BAREBONES.

I follówed the chap with this here varrant, I be's coom'd from Babylon after him.

TÓBY.

Babylon! oh, that mun be in Barkſhire.

BAREBONES.

Great London itſelf. Thou ſeem'ſt ſtrong in fleſh, is the ſpirit with thee?

TÓBY.

Don't vally the devil his ſelf, when I'm doing my duty, no more does my aſſiſtant, Jahn Grum, doeÿ?

JOHN.

Hum!

BAREBONES.

There bee's deſcription of his parſon, (*gives paper.*)

TÓBY.

Meaſter Barleycorn would know if you'll eat dinner at Red Lion.—You may bring company, for we've entertainment for mon and beaſt--An't we Jahn?

JOHN.

Hum!

BAREBONES.

Get a good dinner for me, for I loves to eat and drink of the beſt.

TOBY.

You're a genteel mon---(*apart to John*) Jahn, he'll be as drunk as a tinker, then I comes chalk double on him. Eh, Jahn!

JOHN.

JOHN.

Hum!

[TOBY.

Oh! the Squire, (*looking out.*)

WHIMMY.

(*Without.*) Where did he run---(*Enters*) Oh, you are the canting bawler that broke down one of my ſtatues, (*to Barebones.*)

BAREBONES.

I had an inward call.

WHIMMY.

Curſe your call!

BAREBONES.

He does put it in mine head, with the ſame act, to comfort my fleſh and do a good vork, I vill get myſelf an appetite fore dinner with diſboliſhing this man's idols in his groves and high places.   [*Exit.*

WHIMMY.

If you are ſtill a conſtable, why didn't you take that dangerous leveller into cuſtody?

TOBY.

I munna, he be the planter, and walks at large where he liſt; but I'm going to catch the defender, and I'll bring his body and ſoul before your worſhip, in faſararo.—Come, Jahn!

JOHN.

Hum!   [*Exeunt.*

WHIMMY.

This prancing hermit has fo deranged and jumbled all my fchemes of elegant magnificence---No attention to my old friend Pranks; my daughter not yet prepared to receive his nephew---the final difmiffion not yet given to Peregrine---Lucky that the reft of my houfehold is in train, that all my fervants are fober and regular.----An't this my fine Irifh orator? *(Retires.)*

Enter TULLY *(with a mug in his hand.)*

TULLY.

Upon my foul this hermit is no better than a bad man, that he can't ftay there at his bufinefs, where he has nothing to do but fit quiet---Oh fie, to come here drinking in a public houfe! *(Drinks.)*

Enter CAC HMAN.

WHIMMY.

And my coachman!---

COACHMAN.

Ah! Mafter Tully, I faw you go out at the gate, and fo out of pure good nature I followed you, to give you a little hint, that if Mafter hears you left the gardens to-day, you may chance to lofe your place; befides, coming here to booze is not quite the thing. *(Drinks.)*

WHIMMY.

My daughter's footman too!

Enter SKIP.

SKIP.

Eh, waiter!

Enter

Enter BARLEYCORN (*with a mug.*)

The negus I ordered, a gill of wine, fome water, fugar, and a lemon.

BARLEYCORN.

Why, for wine, I takes out the licence to-morrow; the man is to call next Wednefday with the lemons; my daughter Kitty has loft the key of the fugarcheft; nobody drinks water at Red Lion, fo I have brought you a mug of ale.   [*Exit.*

WHIMMY.

(*Advancing.*) Hey! you fcoundrels, what are you at here with your mugs?

SKIP.

Sir, I came to look for coachman.

COACHMAN.

And I came to bid the gard'ner drive home.

TULLY.

And, Sir, I came after the hermit, becaufe he came before me.

WHIMMY.

You moft ftupid—

TULLY.

Stop, Sir, what fort of talk is that, I'm ftupid? faith, and that's a facret; Sir, Sir Ifaac Newton never found out. Sir, I'm a gard'ner, and though I do dig, I'm not a fpalpeen potatoe-boy—I've read big books of botamy, and the Millar's Dictionary and Cyclopaddy's. Didn't I graft a mayduke uppon a kackagay apple-tree then in my hot-houfe. Didn't my Lord (when he breakfafted with you) pull from the fame tree a cannifter of Hyfon tea and a bafket of Seville oranges? A'n't my flowers fo fweet that the hives round the country are empty, and the fwarms of bees come in a grand congregation into your gardens, humming every body with their bagpipes, fo difcreet all in their black bonnets and their yellow velvet breeches?

WHIMMY.

Men! rafcals! I wifh I could, like the Great Mogul, be attended only by women. Ay, one comfort, my female fervants are diligent and fober.

TULLY.

Faith, Sir, and here's the head of your female fervants coming in very fober here; but how fhe'll get out, for I don't think her bufinefs here is to drink tea.

MRS. MAGGS.

(*Without.*) I will find him. (*Enters.*)

WHIMMY.

Mrs. Maggs, did you want me or my coachman?

MRS. MAGGS.

No, Sir, it was the hermit brought me here.

WHIMMY.

Why, I think——

MRS. MAGGS.

Yes, Sir, I know you think.

WHIMMY.

'Twas the hermit brought us all here.

MRS. MAGGS.

He's come after Kitty—and my love for him is—

TULLY.

He's a ramping devil.

YOUNG PRANKS (*without.*)

(*Singing.*) " With cockle fhell on hat brim."

TULLY.

TULLY.

There he hops over the bufh like a jackdaw.

WHIMMY.

Stop him!
                    [*Exeunt all but Whimmy and Mrs Maggs.*
What vexations! Now, my dear Mrs. Maggs, I've
found out that Tully is a worthlefs man, my whole
dependence of fhewing my fine place is upon you.

MRS. MAGGS.

Now that is fo like Mr. Olmondle.
                    [*Exit Whimmy haftily.*
Blefs me! here comes this moft delightful young man.
I proteft his very approach brings all my blood up in
my face, my heart throbs,—and my limbs—I'm fuch
a poor creature—fo faint—I muft fit, (*goes into a
porch at the door.*)

Enter YOUNG PRANKS.

YOUNG PRANKS.

Come out there, you moft delicate lovelinefs, my
darling rofe bud.

MRS. MAGGS.

(*Rifes and appears.*) Oh, dear Sir—(*fimpering.*)

YOUNG PRANKS.

By the lord, this is my little pitcher again.

KITTY.

(*Unfeen, whips out of the door, and taps him on the
fhoulder.*) Mr. Thomas!

MRS. MAGGS.

A'n't you afhamed of yourfelf, Kitty Barleycorn?

L 2   YOUNG

YOUNG PRANKS.

Come, my dear creatures, you muftn't---

MRS. MAGGS.

Well, I know we muftn't---

YOUNG PRANKS.

What, Ma'am? Don't quarrel about me, zounds ¡
I'm like a ftately peacock between a pheafant and a
turkey hen.

KITTY.

La ! you're fo wild---

MRS. MAGGS.

But he's very merry, he ! he ! he !

YOUNG PRANKS.

Wild ! merry ! my whole life has been one frolic.

MRS. MAGGS.

Ay, I dare fay, when you were a boy---

YOUNG PRANKS.

Such diverfions ! altering the numbers of doors
to puzzle the poftman, at Chriftmas in a ftage coach
changing the directions of geefe, hares, and turkeys,
with a bit of chalk and charcoal making a whole
room of family portraits fquint down upon every
body.

MRS. MAGGS.

I vow you muft not come and fee our pictures.

KITTY.

La ! he's fo pleafant ! Well, and ah, Mr. Tom !

YOUNG

YOUNG PRANKS.

My fweet creature, I came to hanfel the filver cup. Hey! a bottle of port and a roafted orange! Ladies, I vow on the honour of a hermit, I'll treat you with a bifhop. [*Exit into houfe.*

KITTY.

Toby! (*calling.*)

Enter OLD PRANKS.

OLD PRANKS.

Eh! where's this young dog my prentice, bad as my mad nephew. Waiter! my horfe.

MRS. MAGGS.

Sir, you'll return to fup at our houfe.

OLD PRANKS.

Foolifh Dick Whimmy to have no dinner! plague of his gardens, in his ponds plenty of carp and tench, that nobody dare fling into a frying-pan; on his green flopes, neither grafs lamb nor afparagus, and for flocks of geefe and chickens, there a peacock ftruts, or an eagle perches, that inftead of any body eating him, by the Lord, looks as if he'd eat us. My dear, I'm going to Weymouth, cou'dn't you give one a fnack.

KITTY.

Oh! our bill of fare, Sir, (*going.*)

OLD PRANKS.

(*Stops her.*) As fine a bill of fare as e'er I look'd on, (*gazing*) what difh fhall I choofe-- a white forehead, a brace of black eyes, garnifh'd with long
aubu..

auburn eye-lafhes, two rofy cheeks, cherry lips, my defert.

KITTY.

A pity, Mr. Thomas, to difguife his fine hair and delightful fhape, in that long old beard and gown. La! Sir, what a choice hermit you'd make for Mr. Whimmy; you'd be a nice bald-headed buck, as Tom fays.

OLD PRANKS.

I a bald-headed buck! don't you fee I wear my own hair, child?

Re-enter YOUNG PRANKS.

YOUNG PRANKS.

I've brew'd the bifhop. Eh! what old fellow--- fo fmooth with Kitty---Sir, a word if you pleafe, (*twitches off Old Pranks's wig*)---Zounds, my uncle! (*runs off.*)

OLD PRANKS.

Stop that fcoundrel, (*runs after him.*)
[*Bell rings violently, Kitty runs into the houfe.*

Enter MAGGS *walking haftily.*

MRS. MAGGS.

Oh, Heavens! my fon Natty!

MAGGS.

Mamma! fhe has me, but I won't be difgrac'd, (*afide, and turns.*)

MRS. MAGGS.

My dear child, who could think of feeing you down here, (*he turns from her, and walks.*)

MAGGS.

Any bufinefs with me, Ma'am?

MRS. MAGGS.

Why, my dear! Don't you know me, Natty?

MAGGS.

Zounds, Ma'am, don't Natty me!

MRS. MAGGS.

Won't you fpeak to your mother?

MAGGS.

Who are you talking to, Ma'am?

MRS. MAGGS.

Look at me---my own child deny me, (*puts her handkerchief to her eyes, and walks up.*)

Enter TOBY *and* JOHN GRUM.

TOBY.

John, is that the young man you faw?

JOHN.

Hum!

MAGGS.

(*Looking at his watch.*) I fhall be late with my party, (*going.*)

MRS. MAGGS.

Stay, my dear boy!

MAGGS.

MAGGS.

I'm nobody's boy, but my own man, he! he!

TOBY.

Seize him, *(to John)* Your name? *(to Maggs.)*

MAGGS.

What of it?

TOBY.

What is it?

MAGGS.

What it was yefterday, and will be to-morrow.

TOBY.

Mind how he fhuffles; do ye fee it, John? Tell me your name to-morrow, *(to Maggs.)*

MAGGS.

Mufn't, becaufe of mamma. *(afide.)*

TOBY.

You belong to Mr. Pranks.

MAGGS.

Suppofing fo.

TOBY.

Then I fuppofe you're my prifoner.

MAGGS.

Me! for what!

TOBY.

You broke out of jail in Babylon, but we'll hand-cuff and fend you to Dorchefter.

I   MAGGS,

MAGGS.

(*Afide.*) Handcuff! Broke jail in Babylon! Ay! why furely they take me for Tom Pranks!—I'm not the perfon you want.

TOBY.

I arreft you.

MAGGS.

I'm not the man indeed, my friend.

TOBY.

Who anfwers for you? who knows you?

MAGGS.

Then I muft own mother---let me go, this gen-tlewoman here is my honour'd mamma.

MRS. MAGGS.

(*Afide.*) A wicked wretch, firft to deny, and now to own me in his diftrefs!

TOBY.

Mrs. Maggs, be he your fon?

MRS. MAGGS.

Oh! no, he's no fon of mine.

MAGGS.

Nay, my dear mamma.

MRS. MAGGS.

Sir, don't mamma me; who are you talking to? (*mimicking.*)

MAGGS.

Ay! why fure, fweet mamma!---

M   TOBY.

TOBY.

Stop; you fee, my friend, it won't pafs. John, look he don't run away, while I read difcription of his parfon, (*takes out paper and reads*) five feet eight inches tall, an expreffive eye, pleafing features, good complexion, fine teeth, fhew your teeth, (*to Maggs*) a handfome countenance---

MAGGS.

'Pon my foul this defcription's very much like me tho'.

TOBY.

Well-made, a genteel deportment; upon the whole, an elegant figure.

MAGGS.

Amazing! what a picture of me!

MRS. MAGGS.

Aftonifhing like the child indeed.

TOBY.

You fee it's you.

MAGGS.

No, it's fuch another handfome fellow, but really not me.

TOBY.

Come, I arreft you with a little tap, (*trips up his heels*) hold his legs, Jahn, that he mayn't kick I.

MAGGS.

Damn'd uncivil this!

MRS.

MRS. MAGGS.

I can't bear to fee him treated fo---let the child go, you fellows!

TOBY.

Yes, the child fhall go---to prifon.

MRS. MAGGS.

You're wrong, he's my fon.

TOBY.

And juft now you faid—Ay, I fee how 'tis, Meafter Butler told me that Mrs. Maggs locks herfelf in her own room, and there drinks the prefarved apricocks—Jahn don't mind, Madam Maggs is fo fond of talking fhe'll fay any thing---bring him along.

MAGGS.

Sir, gentlemen conftables! mamma! kind country juftices! mother! (*Toby holding him by the head, and John by the legs, they drag him off.*)

MRS. MAGGS.

Why, you horrid villains, you fhall not!—my child! [*Exit after them.*

SCENE III. *The Gardens. Statues thrown down, and broken fragments lying about ; fhrubs and plants, as pulled up.*

Enter BAREBONES, (*with a broken ftatue.*)

BAREBONES.

I vill complete the good work ; lay there accurfed, (*throws it down on a heap*) and I vill pulls

M 2   up

up thy groves, and I vill root thee out of the land, (*pulls plants out of pots, and flings them about.*)

Enter BARLEYCORN.

BARLEYCORN.

Sir, your dinner's waiting. (*Aside*) Dang my buttons! here's a fine kick-up! what rascal cou'd have got in here—some one that owes the 'squire a grudge.

BAREBONES.

I've been doing of the job, 'twas all pagan wanity.

BARLEYCORN.

So it was, Sir, and you were right to capsize it.

Enter KITTY.

KITTY.

Oh! father, I shall go distracted; I'm sure it's my belov'd Tom that they're taking pris'ner to Dorchester, yet so cruel not to let me see him.

Enter TOBY.

TOBY.

I've left the prisoner in safe custody with Jahn Grum.

BAREBONES.

(*Aside.*) Then I brings him up to town, and lodges him with the Marshal.

KITTY.

Oh heaven! tell me, Toby, is it the hermit?

TOBY.

TOBY.

No.

KITTY.

It is he.

TOBY.

'Tis not tho'—why you're as bad as Mrs. Maggs, who juft now faid he was her fon, and he wasn't her fon—there's difcription of his perfon, (*gives Kitty a a paper.*)

KITTY.

(*Reading with emotion.*)   Handfome, elegant, fine teeth, expreffive eye—'tis he! you hard-hearted creature—but I'll releafe my own true love, tho' I beg my bread for it.   [*Exit haftily.*

TOBY.

Ay now, fhe too has been drinking apricocks.— Be's I to lay the cloth for you in the two-bedded room, (*to Barebones.*)

BAREBONES.

I loves to eat in a parlour.

BARLEYCORN.

Why we wifh to refarve that for—

TOBY.

Parlour! than, Sir, fhan't I tap no vind—he won't inform—(*to Barleycorn.*)

BAREBONES.

I drinks vind, for I thirfts after the good things of this world.

BARLEYCORN.

That's right.

2   TOBY.

TOBY.

He's a wet Chriſtian.

BARLEYCORN.

Shall they take up dinner?

BAREBONES.

Yes, I hungers after good; I could munch one morcil of Portlin mutton; yea, one pound and an half, and ſix, and four, and two wheat ears, roaſted in wine leaves, and other ſettries of niceiſh ſaver.

[*Exit with Toby.*

BARLEYCORN.

(*Looking out.*) The 'ſquire—dang my buttons, here'll be work.   [*Exit.*

Enter WHIMMY, (*looks at the broken Statues with amazement.*)

WHIMMY.

Fury and diſtraction! what's all here!—Tully! (*calls.*)

Enter TULLY, (*a little intoxicated.*)

TULLY.

(*Singing.*) " They'd be like the Highlanders eating of kail,
     " And curſing the Union, ſays Granawaile."

WHIMMY.

This is your going to the alehouſe, here's your brags, here's yellow-breech'd bees humming their bag-pipes—but I'll turn over a new leaf, I'll dig and root out—

TULLY.

Arrah, Sir, I wiſh you'd let the leaves and the trees alone! you've been digging and rooting pret-
tily:

tily : what put it into your head to pull up the plants in this manner ?

WHIMMY.

My head, there's my dancing Faunus.

TULLY.

Oh ! I fee how this is ; you want to keep me only as your fhow-man, and take the head gard'ning into your own hands—the geranums all torn, the myrtles, and lillies, and laylocks, are all pull'd about as if they were old bean ftalks.

WHIMMY.

You rafcal ! what do you talk of your paltry plants—look at my ftatues, 'none equal to them in the Barbarini gallery.

TULLY.

The barber's gallery ! Only tell a body what you intend to put down in the place—if yourfelf was planted, the devil a thing would grow out of your head but potatoe apples.

WHIMMY.

Two of my Seafons—

TULLY.

You don't know the feafons ; you're a gentleman, and you've money to buy roots and fruits, but I tell you, you don't know an annual from an ever-green. I got myfelf finely laughed at to-day by fhowing your kickfhaws, but I wafh my hands out of it. There's your defcribing book (*throws book down*) and you may get another Ciceroni magpye to chatter to the company. [*Exit.*

WHIMMY.

WHIMMY.

There's a villain !

Enter OLD PRANKS.

OLD PRANKS.

Knock people's hats off—can't think who the fellow was !—Dick, I'm on the fpur to fetch my nephew from Weymouth ; an idle fcoundrel ! what perplexities he has involved me in ! Dolts to apprehend Natty Maggs for him ; thefe country conftables are fo obftinate, won't even take my word : but what fort of wild people have you fettled amongft here that pull folks heads about ?

WHIMMY.

Yes, heads, legs, and arms, look ! (*points to the ftatues.*)

OLD PRANKS.

(*Looking round.*) Ha ! ha ! ha ! a good deed, however.

WHIMMY.

What, to demolifh my beauties ?

OLD PRANKS.

Your modern gardens are art fpoiling nature ; fixing up a ftone woman where one expects to find a rofy girl of health, flefh, and blood : if we muft have ftatues, inftead of importing ancient heathen gods into Englifh meadows, why not encourage Britifh arts to celebrate Britifh heroes ? for a Jupiter by Phidias give me an Elliot by a Bacon : the five thoufand pounds you laid out upon that clumfy Pantheon yonder, wou'd have built a neat clufter of alms-houfes, where age and infancy might find an afylum from the pangs of indigence.

WHIMMY.

WHIMMY.

Why, but Billy---

OLD PRANKS.

'Sblood, when I reflect I owe my prefent independence to my education in the Blue Coat School, as I drive my whifky on a Sunday by Dulwich College, I feel more warmth of affection for the memory of Edward the king, or Alleyn the player, than for all the travelling cognofcenti in Chriftendom. Dick, I love reafon.

Enter YOUNG PRANKS.

YOUNG PRANKS.

A rare chace, but I got from him---zounds! (*fees Old Pranks, runs off.*)

OLD PRANKS.

Oh, damme, I'll have you, (*purfues.*)

WHIMMY.

He likes reafon, and the fellow's mad; there he runs after my hermit. Certainly 'twas this favage old Goth committed thefe barbarifms—I hope he'll not find his nephew; however, I muft prepare my daughter for the marriage. [*Exit.*

SCENE III. *Infide of Hermitage.* YOUNG PRANKS *fitting in his Hermit's Drefs, as if put on haftily.*

Enter OLD PRANKS.

OLD PRANKS.

(*Looking about.*) I thought I had a glimpfe of him darting this way—Eh! one of Whimmy's toys

N   (*fee-*

---(_feeing Young Pranks_) Father Dominick---feen a
fcoundrel run in here—Do ye hear! can you fpeak!
—it was certainly my nephew; a hound! fkulking
about, and fuffer a poor innocent man to be taken
up for him; to be handcuff'd, haul'd, and dragg'd—

YOUNG PRANKS.

An innocent man fuffer for me! (_throws off his
hermit's drefs._)

OLD PRANKS.

You! Oh you villain! How dare you borrow
money about as you have done!

YOUNG PRANKS.

Sir, (_confufed_) I—I—borrow'd money to get out
of debt.

OLD PRANKS.

Eh! how?

YOUNG PRANKS.

Yes, Sir, to pay my debts.

OLD PRANKS.

But why get in debt?

YOUNG PRANKS.

All owing to my good principle, the people
wou'd truft me, my character was fo excellent.

OLD PRANKS.

Then from your excellent character they think you
a damn'd rogue—you villain!

YOUNG PRANKS.

Dear Sir, difcriminate between vice and folly;
you are the only one I ever wrong'd, my fecond
parent,

parent, my friend, my benefactor. Sooner than let
this perfon you fpoke of juft now any longer bear
the difgrace that I only deferve, I'll inftantly free
him by delivering myfelf up to hopelefs imprifonment, (*going*.)

OLD PRANKS.

Eh! ftop you rogue you, confider how terrible a
prifon is.

YOUNG PRANKS.

Lord, Sir, no! the only difference between the
people walking by and I is, that they're on one
fide of the door and I'm on t'other. A prifon! to
refign myfelf to it, now, is barely performing the
duties of honefty.   [*Exit*.

OLD PRANKS.

Surrenders to free the guiltlefs! Not fo bad as I
thought him.

Enter KITTY.

KITTY.

Sir, I've been told, fince you're a banker gentleman in Lombard-ftreet, London, you bankers,
Sir, have always a great deal of money.

OLD PRANKS.

(*Afide*.) I've heard of petticoat pads—a piftol may
come out here! Well, my dear, granting I have
money, do you want any?

KITTY.

Not myfelf, Sir; there's a young gentleman is
taken up for debt, Sir; I thought it a pity he
fhould go to prifon, as he got out of it before, and
that,

that, you know, Sir, is a fign he doesn't like it; hard for a perfon to go where they can't be happy.

OLD PRANKS.

Upon my word this young lady reafons exceeding pretty---Well, Mifs?

KITTY.

And Sir, my aunt by mother's fide, has left me three hundred pounds independent of my father. here are the papers, Sir, all about it, Sir, if you'd be fo kind as to advance the money, and tranfact the bufinefs of releafing the young gentleman with it, I'd be very much obliged to you, Sir, (*curtfies.*)

OLD PRANKS.

Here's a charming girl! And fo, my dear, you think Natty Maggs fo fine a fellow, that you give up all your fortune to releafe him.

KITTY.

Natty Maggs! No, Sir, our 'fquire's hermit.

OLD PRANKS.

Hermit! She muft mean my wild nephew, (*over-joyed.*)

KITTY.

Sir, keep the papers, I know you'll free him; you look fo good-natured, I befeech you, Sir, Sir,
[*curtfies and exit.*

OLD PRANKS.

Tol lol lol, (*fings.*) The heart of an amiable woman is the true touchftone of manly merit. This good and delicate treature loves my nephew, and he muft be a worthy lad. The girl, no matter for
her

her fituation, is come of a good ftock, and fhould
be tranfplanted. I didn't, till now, know my
nephew.--I'll forgive, I'll give him all---Go to the
King's Bench again! that he fhan't, while I've a guinea to keep him out of it, tol lol lol. [*Sings and exit,*

SCENE IV. *A Gallery in Whimmy's Houfe.*

Enter YOUNG PRANKS (*haftily croffing*) *and* PERE-
GRINE *meeting,* (*much egitated.*)

PEREGRINE.

Stop, Tom, whither now?

YOUNG PRANKS

To the King's Bench---what's the matter? Oh,
true, Mifs Dian told me---upon ny foul her father
ufes you both very ill—who is this vhelp he is going
to give her to?

PEREGRINE.

I don't know; Mr. Whimmy has never even
feen him.

YOUNG PRANKS.

No! An uncle, isn't it that's briging this about?
I've a good uncle---but long befoe he'd think of
providing me with an heirefs---bit then I've been
fuch a curfed fellow.

PEREGRINE.

One chance, this fpark may, as i's a forced thing,
be indifferent, and the old gentleran doats fo upon
his

his daughter, that were an emperor to flight her, 'twou'd for ever lofe his favour.

YOUNG PRANKS.

What's this uncle's name ?—who, where, what is he ?

PEREGRINE.

I know nothing about him.

YOUNG PRANKS.

Nor old Whimmy neither.

PEREGRINE.

I've never feen him, I told you.

YOUNG PRANKS.

Then I'll perfonate him, and I warrant you difguift the old gentlman fufficiently to make him break off the match ; then, Peregrine, is your harveft. I'll be with you n a trice.   Never be difmay'd, Peregrine, when you admit me as a fchemer into your cabinet ; for I hive turn'd my coat fo often fince I arriv'd in thefe parts, that there is no doubt of my being a moft finfhed politician.   [*Exit.*

Enter WIIMMY *and* DIAN, *weeping.*

WHIMMY.

In vain talkng, child;—I muft keep my firft promife.

DIAN.

But, dear Si will you fentence your child to mifery ?

PEREGRINE.

Sir, you encourag'd me with a certainty that I fhou'd be the happieft of men, and now in a moment, to fnatch me from Heaven, and plunge me into an abyfs of defpair.

WHIMMY.

Can't help it, Dian;—I muft give you to my friend's nephew.

Enter SKIP.

SKIP.

Sir, here's a young gentleman will fee you—feems in a pitcous taking. Here's my mafter, Sir.

(Calling off.)

Enter YOUNG PRANKS, *difguifed like a boy, his hair pulled round his face, &c.*

YOUNG PRANKS, *(crying.)*

Oh! I will not have her.

WHIMMY.

Ah! who are you?

PEREGRINE.

Certainly Tom Pranks. *(To Dian.)*

WHIMMY.

What do you want?

YOUNG PRANKS.

I don't want a wife. *(Roars out crying.)*

WHIMMY.

. WHIMMY.

Who the devil cares, whether you do or no— have you any bufinefs?

YOUNG PRANKS.

No; I'm a gentleman. My uncle fays I muft marry your daughter; but I won't. *(Roaring out.)*

WHIMMY.

Ah! can this be the wild rogue I've heard fo much of? why, your uncle told me you were an-other-guefs being. Dian, this is your hufband.— How do you like him?

DIAN, *(apart to Peregrine.)*

I fee this. Sir, if Mr. Peregrine can pardon me, . fince you've fet your heart on't, I'm refign'd to your will, with the dutiful obedience of a daughter.
(Curtfies.)

WHIMMY.

Now, that's very lucky. Peregrine, you fee—

PEREGRINE.

Then, Sir, fince the lady is fo very fickle, I re-fign her with little regret.

WHIMMY.

Ah! this is all very well; then we'll call your uncle; Parfon Jack is in the next room, and you fhall be married immediately.

YOUNG PRANKS.

But I won't marry, oh! *(cries)*—I'll never fay, father-in-law, to fuch an ugly old fellow as you.

WHIMMY.

WHIMMY.

Why, you damn'd impudent young fcoundrel, dare you affront me, and refufe my daughter ? then let your uncle do his worft. There, Peregrine, take Dian, and may I be curs'd if ever I again attempt to part you.

PEREGRINE.

You'll alter your mind again, Sir.

WHIMMY.

I'll put that out of my power—go, Doctor, (*calling off*) tack that couple together inftantly.

(Puts Dian and Peregrine off.)

Enter OLD PRANKS.

YOUNG PRANKS.

My uncle ! oh ! zounds !

WHIMMY.

Billy, what bouncing you've kept about this ne-phew of your's. He, a buck, and a blood !—a blubbering milkfop.

OLD PRANKS.

My Tom a milkfop ! I fay he's a buck.

WHIMMY.

I fay he's an afs. *(Wrangling, Y. Pranks cries out.)*

WHIMMY.

There's the buck ! a taftelefs hound, has been abufing me here, and refufed my daughter.

O   YOUNG

YOUNG PRANKS.

Oh! the devil! am I really the character I only perfonated. *(Afide.)*

OLD PRANKS.

Where is he?

WHIMMY.

Can't you fee? thrafh him for his impudence to me.

OLD PRANKS.

Why, ah, Tom!

YOUNG PRANKS.

Aye, poor Tom! *(Snivelling.)*

WHIMMY.

By the Lord, it's my galloping hermit! *(furpris'd)* and your nephew.

YOUNG PRANKS. *(To Old Pranks.)*

Sir, I now fee your goodnefs; but had I even before known it, I cou'd not have enjoy'd the blefling you defign'd for me, at the expence of a friend's happinefs. Mr. Peregrine has love and merit.—I admire, but don't deferve the lady.

OLD PRANKS.

Then, fince you're fo difinterefted as to decline the golden pippin, I'll give you a fweet wild ftrawberry.

Enter KITTY.

KITTY.

O Mr. Banker, have you—'tis he *(looking at Young Pranks with joy)* thanky, Sir. *(Curtfies to Old Pranks.)*

OLD

OLD PRANKS.

Tom, here's a girl that wou'd have barter'd all her little fortune for your freedom; and now as you hope for mine, take her.

WHIMMY.

Why, fhe's daughter to the Red Lion.

OLD PRANKS.

Aye, my honeft landlord, that reliev'd the fufferers, while you were fwallowing peaches in December, and the poor fhivering in cold and nakednefs. Red Lion, Dick! where honour's derived from benevolence; fhe's daughter to a nobleman. What fay you, my girl?

KITTY.

Only, Sir, that my heart is fill'd with gratitude; but you muft afk the Red Lion's confent; for tho' you were a hufband for a queen, I wou'd not have a prince, if it might grieve an indulgent parent.

Enter TOBY *and* JOHN GRUM, *with* MAGGS, *(his drefs very much difordered and torn.)*

TOBY.

Your worfhip, here's the defender is obftropolos, and has lick'd I and John Grum.

MAGGS.

Aye, dem'me, I plump'd 'em.

YOUNG PRANKS.

Was't you, Natty? I'm forry that my irregularities fhou'd have involv'd you in this trouble.

Ente

Enter Mrs. MAGGS.

MRS. MAGGS.

Oh! Natty Maggs---my child to be haul'd and maul'd---but this comes of your denying me your honour'd mother.

OLD PRANKS.

Haul'd and maul'd—may the fon never get better ufage who cou'd deny his parent.

Enter BARLEYCORN *and* TULLY, *bringing in* BARE-BONES.

BARLEYCORN.

Dang my buttons, you fhall—

WHIMMY.

What's this?

TULLY.

Only this devout preacher walks into Mr. Barley-corn's and crams himfelf like a great fowl; then walks off without difcharging his fhot; when afk'd, fays he, you'll be paid above, and fays Mr. Barley-corn, by who there? and fays he, why by Abdiel; fo they walk'd up ftairs to me, where I was taking a pint and a whiff of tobacco. I was chriften'd Mr. Tully; fo I walks down---but who ever faw an angel with a pipe in his mouth? I don't mind paying for a man's dinner; but, Sir, be fo kind as to fend this gentleman to jail. How do ye do, Mrs. Maggs?

(Bowing.)

YOUNG

YOUNG PRANKS.

My Saint George's Fields landlord!

BAREBONES.

The ſpirit openeth my mouth.

TULLY.

You opened your mouth to ſwallow a leg of lamb, honey.

BAREBONES.

All things ſhall be in common with the righteous?

TOBY.

Pay me for ſarving capias on Muſter Pranks.

YOUNG PRANKS.

Me! how?

OLD PRANKS.

Capias! What, you villain, are you that Ham Barebones that has lent my nephew money at an exorbitant uſance.

YOUNG PRANKS.

That, like the devil, tempted me by the means, and now puniſhes me for the ſin.

TULLY.

Talk of righteouſneſs! and bilk the houſe of an honeſt induſtrious man. (*Lays bold on Barebones.*)

Enter

Enter PEREGRINE *and* DIAN.

PEREGRINE.

Mrs. Peregrine (*to Whimmy.*)

DIAN.

Deareſt father, your bleſſing. (*They kneel to Whimmy.*)

TULLY.

There, my bleſſing on you both, you two ſouls. (*Puts his hand on their heads.*)

YOUNG PRANKS.

Then, my dear uncle, I take my lovely Kitty Barleycorn, and whilſt her gentle qualities convince our friends, that birth and rank are not neceſſary to conſtitute an amiable wife, my reſpect for her virtues may prove, that the thoughtleſs prodigal can make a good huſband.

WHIMMY.

Oh! I'm happy! ha! ha! ha! We've all got ſo very generous. Peregrine, with his little fortune, have Dian and all my wealth; your nephew, with your riches, takes little Kitty Barleycorn with nothing at all; and ecod, Mrs. Maggs looks ſo ſpruce, that I could find in my heart to—(*going up to her.*)

MRS. MAGGS.

Now that's ſo like Mr. Olmondle, (*ſmiling and advancing.*)

WHIMMY.

Oh! (*runs from her.*)

I

TULLY.

And now, Mrs. Maggs, you will be drinking the apricocks.

YOUNG PRANKS.

Then, Sir, ſhall we be merry. Here ends my ſeven years hermitage, and, inſtead of my annuity, I ſhall think myſelf nobly rewarded, if my extravagant tricks and fancies can, by an indulgent ſmile, receive the forgiveneſs of my generous friends.

F I N I S.

www.ingramcontent.com/pod-product-compliance
Lightning Source LLC
Chambersburg PA
CBHW022144020726
47496CB00008B/2555